MY LADY, MY SPY
SECRETS AND SEDUCTION

SHERIDAN JEANE

F&F
Flowers and Fiction

For my family.
Both the ones created through blood bonds and the ones forged through life experience. You mean the world to me.

L*ondon, January 6, 1854*
     "Do you think the Russians——" Josephine stopped speaking mid-sentence the moment she caught sight of Frederick Woolsy weaving through the crowded ballroom. She'd recognize his dark hair and the way his tall form moved anywhere... even in a sea of men wearing black formal coats. What was he doing here at the Koliada Ball? He'd sent her a message only this morning saying he wasn't coming. Surely he hadn't lied to her. He wouldn't have.

Would he?

She hated that she doubted him, even for an instant.

"Lady Harrington? Is something wrong?"

"What?" She dragged her attention back to her friend and gave him a distracted smile. She'd momentarily forgotten about him. "The embassy is appallingly warm, Tristan. I wonder if the Russians are in the habit of overheating their rooms. I find myself quite parched." She licked her dry lips.

A flicker of a frown crossed Tristan's face. Did he suspect she wanted to send him away on some useless errand simply to rid herself of him? If so, his good breeding prevented him from saying anything. "Would you permit me to bring you some punch?"

She smiled her thanks. "That would be splendid."

Josephine waited until he disappeared from sight and then hurried toward a spot where she could intercept Frederick and his brother. She was only halfway there when the Duchess of Eckley stepped in her path, barring her progress.

Fiddlesticks. There was nothing like a duchess with a determined gleam in her eye to put one's plans in a muddle.

The young duchess's eyes were bright with excitement. "I'm so glad I found you," she said. "You're acquainted with Mr. Woolsy, are you not?"

"You know I am," Josephine replied, frowning. She hoped she wasn't blushing.

The duchess's lips barely twitched as she raked her gaze over Josephine, taking in every detail of her celadon-blue gown. "Did you hear about the dreadful accident? It's quite shocking. Lord Tamworth and Mr. Woolsy were injured in a fire on the patio. It happened only a few minutes ago. Poor Lord Tamworth's injuries are rather severe. He's being whisked away in his carriage even as we speak."

Josephine gasped. "That's horrible. Are you certain the second man was Mr. Woolsy? I just saw him with Lord Wentworth, and he didn't appear to be injured."

"Quite certain," Lady Eckley said, "but Mr. Woolsy's burns are said to be relatively minor in comparison to poor Lord Tamworth's."

Josephine glanced across the room to the spot where she'd last seen Frederick and caught sight of him entering the grand foyer. Now that she knew what to look for, he did seem slightly curled in on himself as though in pain. He held his right hand protectively against his chest and cradled a white bundle of cloth. Perhaps a bandage?

"That's dreadful," Josephine said. "How did it happen?"

Lady Eckley pursed her lips in disapproval. "It was that oaf, Lord Percival. He's three sheets to the wind tonight. He managed to knock over an oil lamp and set an entire table on fire."

Josephine shook her head. "That man is a menace."

"Yes, I—oh, there's the ambassador. I simply must find out what he plans to do about their misfortune. He's the host, after all. He bears some responsibility." She darted away before Josephine could say another word.

Josephine searched the room for Frederick but couldn't find him. For a moment, she considered forgetting she'd seen him. He'd abandoned her all week, leaving her doubting where she stood. She let out a frustrated sigh. This would be her best opportunity to speak with him. She couldn't let it slip away.

With nothing more than a glance, Frederick Woolsy had the power to make her feel like a débutante rather than a widow, which she found most unsettling. Most unsettling indeed. Following her husband's sudden and pointless death in a hunting mishap, marriage no longer held any particular interest for her. Never again would she consent to be tied to a man she barely knew.

But her opinion on the matter had undergone a reversal one short week ago.

In one night, Frederick had managed to alter her thinking on the subject. One memorable night.

An undeniable attraction toward one another had drawn them together over the past few months. When she'd finally agreed to the tryst at Lord Saxon's country house last weekend, they'd been discreet. No one guessed that Frederick had crept into her room both nights.

Both blissful nights.

Frederick had been a divine lover. Skilled and caring. Thinking about him now allowed images from that night to invade her mind. She almost gasped as her toes began to curl in her dancing shoes.

Her. Curling toes. Ridiculous! Widows shouldn't have curling toes.

She set off toward the grand foyer to search for him, weaving her way between the guests as she followed the path he'd taken.

In the bedroom, the late Lord Harrington had been nothing like Frederick. John believed a lady should abhor sexual intercourse. Apparently, she was supposed to find it base and beneath her. One night early in their marriage she'd almost enjoyed having marital relations with him, but he'd pulled away from her and called her wanton and unnatural. After that, she'd learned to suppress any enjoyment in their intimacy, but that hadn't been particularly difficult. He only came into her bed briefly to perform his duty, as he referred to it, and once the act was complete, he quickly escaped back to his own chambers.

The nights with Frederick had been a revelation. He'd actually *wanted* her to find pleasure in their union. In fact, he'd withheld his own release until he'd helped her find her own. The experience had been eye-opening. And toe-curling.

He'd also introduced her to an item she'd only heard mentioned in scandalized whispers. A French letter—a mere slip of a thing to cover a man's—well—his most private part. He said it would prevent her from becoming pregnant. They'd used a number of them over those two nights. More than she'd imagined possible.

He'd left her bed that last morning with kisses and plans and promises, but had avoided her ever since. She hadn't seen him in a week.

Not until tonight.

Josephine finally escaped the crowded ballroom and entered the foyer. She looked around, but found no sign of Frederick *or* his brother. They'd both disappeared.

Movement above her on the balcony caught her attention. Was that Frederick? It was! And when he spotted her, he ducked out of sight. But she'd seen him. Of that she was certain.

Why had he gone up there? Was he merely curious about the

embassy's renovations? She dismissed the idea. There was more than mere curiosity driving his actions.

She moved toward the staircase, intending to follow him, but a large footman stepped in front of her, blocking the way.

"Upstairs area is restricted," the man said in a thick Russian accent. "No guests allowed."

Josephine glanced at the balcony again, but couldn't spot Frederick. She knew better than to mention his flouting of the rules to the footman. Frederick must have evaded him by taking an alternate route upstairs.

She acquiesced and stepped away, glancing around the grand foyer. She spotted a door on the far side of the room leading toward the embassy offices. It wasn't guarded. Perhaps she'd find another staircase back there.

A children's choir began singing. The other guests around her moved to watch them. As a group passed between her and the man guarding the staircase, Josephine slipped through a side door and found herself in a corridor lined with embassy offices. There should be another, less opulent staircase nearby—a route for the servants.

The office doors were all closed, but about halfway down the hallway she noticed one standing slightly ajar. She hurried closer to open it and grinned when she discovered the servants' staircase, just as she'd predicted.

Josephine lifted the hem of her skirt and crept up the stairs. Her night would end in disaster if she ran into one of the embassy's servants. Those Russian footmen looked intimidating.

She paused when she reached the landing. The door leading to the corridor was closed, but she heard someone moving on the other side of it. She paused as she tried to identify the odd shuffling sound. Whatever it was, it seemed to be moving away from her.

Cautiously, she edged the door open and peeked into the hallway. A man was sliding a cloth along the floor with his shoe, wiping up what appeared to be water.

Not just any man. *Frederick.*

She pushed open the door and stepped through.

At the sound, he spun to face her. His jaw dropped as his piercing blue eyes widened in surprise. "Josephine? What in blazes are you doing up here?"

"You canceled our plans for tonight. Imagine my surprise when you strolled through the ballroom." She gave him a frigid smile. "Shall I give you an opportunity to explain yourself before I set the dogs on you, or will you only use it to lie to me again?"

❦

FREDERICK STARED AT JOSEPHINE IN ASTONISHMENT AS SHE glared at him. Her exquisiteness stole his breath away for a moment—her pale blond hair, her lush form in her signature shade of celadon blue, her angry blue eyes that crackled with recrimination. She was a vision, yes—but not a welcome one. At least, not at this precise moment.

She must have followed him.

Her gaze raked over him. He had the sense she didn't miss anything. "What are you doing with that cloth?"

He glanced down at the rag he'd been using to clean the floor and was startled into giving her an honest answer. "I dripped a trail of water down the hallway and now I'm wiping it up."

"Water?"

He lifted his hand, which was wrapped in sodden cloth. "This used to contain a bundle of ice."

Her angry expression softened. "I heard you were burned. Is it a serious injury?"

"Serious enough."

Her forehead furrowed with concern as she moved closer. "May I see?"

"You shouldn't be up here. It isn't safe."

She ignored him and continued to approach. His entire body reacted to her proximity. With effort, he tore his gaze away from her and glanced down the corridor. The water droplets were gone. He'd managed to wipe away all evidence of his presence.

He glanced back and met Josephine's expectant gaze. With a heavy sigh, he lifted the wet cloth from his hand.

She let out a sympathetic hiss of pain, and he glanced down at his hand. He wasn't surprised by the large white blisters on the fingertips of his right hand. The skin around them was an angry red.

She cradled both his hands in hers. Gentle. Careful.

Their connection was immediate. Intense.

Desire coursed through him.

His body knew her.

Wanted her.

Craved her.

She seemed unaware of his reaction as she focused on his left hand. The pads of all every fingertip had been seared by the flames. Even his smallest finger had formed a blister along the outer edge.

Then she turned her attention to his right hand. "Oh, Frederick," she whispered. She grazed her fingertips over his wrist, keeping well away from the burns.

As she let out a sigh, she held her hand above his fingers as though she wanted to touch them, but she withdrew. Even the heat of her skin hovering near the burns had aggravated them, but some perverse part of him relished the pain because it had come from her deep concern for him.

Her gaze met his, her eyes full of anguish. "Have you taken anything for the pain?"

He swallowed. Now that he'd examined his hand, ignoring the pain was becoming more difficult. "A glass of whiskey," he replied. He glanced around nervously and realized they were too close to the balcony. Someone might see them from below. See her. His chest tightened. He couldn't take that chance. What if she were caught? Questioned? He moved closer to the wall, tilting his head for her to join him. "Josephine, you aren't safe here."

"Only one glass? You'll need to drink more than that if you want to dull the pain."

She pushed open the nearest door and didn't hesitate before walking inside. Was she mad?

She turned toward the small table next to the door. With brisk efficiency, she extracted a match from a box she found there, struck it, and lit a candle.

"There must be a decanter of whiskey in here somewhere," she murmured, "or perhaps vodka since this is the Russian embassy." She tipped the candle and used it to light an oil lamp sitting on a dressing table. "Russians are known for their vodka, are they not?"

"What are you doing?" Frederick asked, following her through the doorway. "You can't simply walk into someone's bedroom."

"Fiddlesticks. I'm looking for something for you to drink. I'm sure the ambassador wouldn't object, considering you were injured at his embassy."

The woman was mad. Absolutely mad. But he had to admit there was a certain logic to her argument. What did that say about him?

He took in the room. His gaze danced across the pristine white coverlet on the bed. In a flash, he imagined Josephine draped across the snowy expanse, naked, a smile of invitation curving across her lips. He quickly turned away. How could his mind conjure such carnal images when he was injured, in the middle of an important mission, and at risk of being discovered at any moment?

He forced himself to focus on the room's details. The empty dressing table. The fireplace laid and ready for a match. The leather satchel near the door. Yes, the room was occupied. Probably by a visitor, not a resident, judging by the lack of personal items.

He checked the corridor. Empty. At least they hadn't been spotted. He needed to get rid of Josephine before she attracted the wrong kind of attention. Attention that could ruin his mission and provoke a declaration of war. He gently pushed the door shut with the back of his hand, wincing as the latch made a sharp noise.

She grinned with delight when she spotted a bottle. "Voila! Vodka!"

She splashed a large amount of the clear liquid into a tumbler and handed it to him. "Drink it all," she directed him. "It will help with the pain."

He took it gingerly in his left hand, frowning at the contents. "Not a good idea," he muttered. He needed a clear head. He could bear the pain until he and his brother managed to remove the book they were stealing from the embassy grounds. "I'm not a good drinker. I tend to get maudlin and a bit testy, so I try not to imbibe."

"In that case, I'll remember to avoid you for the rest of the evening. Now, drink it all. I insist."

He frowned at her. Josephine could be stubborn once she'd made up her mind, and he didn't have time to argue with her— not if he wanted her out of here quickly. Given his current situation, submitting to her demand would be the most expedient course of action. Plus, she was right. His hand hurt as though the devil himself had flayed it open. His plan had been compromised. That meant he needed to adjust. Adapt. Improvise.

He took the glass gingerly in his left hand and gave it a disapproving frown. He made a decision and downed the fiery liquid, then contorted his face in distaste. He'd never been fond of spirits.

His sleeve brushed her shoulder as he reached past her to set the tumbler back on the dressing table. Standing so close to her made him pause. The heat from her body filled the space between them, drawing him to her as their eyes met. Lord, this woman was irresistible.

Her lips quivered, and then she gave him a tremulous smile. "You smell of cigars, whiskey, smoke, and bay rum." Her words were forthright, as though they had burst from her without being first considered. He knew from her sharp intake of breath that their close proximity affected her as well.

"Just like every other man who sat outside with Lord Percival tonight." He kept his tone light, even as he breathed her in. Josephine had her own distinctive scent. With her standing so close to him, it invaded him. She smelled of lavender and freesia. She'd once told him she'd had the perfume blended especially for her, which hadn't surprised him at all.

He'd discovered that when they made love, the scent lingered on his skin, even after he'd bathed. At Lord Saxon's country house, it had remained with him all the following day, constantly reminding him of her. Luring him back to her.

He wanted nothing more than to wrap his arms around her now, drag her onto that bed, and relive the time they'd spent together.

Instead, he forced himself to pull back. Restraint might be painful, but it was the wiser course. The more prudent one. Hadn't he already reached this same conclusion earlier this week? He shouldn't involve himself with Josephine. Not her. Not anyone.

He could quash his attraction to her with time. With distance. A strategic retreat. A slow adjustment of the pieces on the board, rather like castling one's king in a chess match.

He needed to stay focused. Both tonight on this mission, and in the future. Josephine deserved a man who would never lie to her—who would be wholly dedicated to her—not a man with split loyalties. He could never be that man.

On their last night together, she'd confessed how much she

detested being lied to, deceived, or manipulated. She'd stared at him as she said it, and the pressure to reveal his secrets had been difficult to ignore, but he hadn't told her.

He couldn't bring himself to confess he was a spy working in the service of Queen Victoria's Foreign Office. That he'd been hiding this from her all along.

Yes, Frederick Woolsy, younger brother to the Earl of Wentworth, was a spy. This information was a carefully guarded secret, and he planned to keep it that way.

He'd been forced to lie to her again and again over the past year, but he'd had little choice. He'd been hard pressed to fabricate excuses for the clandestine meetings, the sudden short jaunts to boring locales, his month-long trips to first Paris and then Edinburgh, his inability to follow through on plans due to last-minute "conflicts." He often put her off by saying "I'll keep you informed" regarding some event she hoped they'd attend together. When duty called, he disappeared like vapor, not even leaving a lingering scent behind.

Why was he tarrying with her now when war was at stake? He should leave.

There was that word again. *Should.*

Josephine picked up a fresh, dry cloth lying next to the washbasin and gently began bandaging his hand with it. "We need to talk about last week."

He blinked. Of course they did. "You're right, but can it wait just a bit longer? I need to find my brother. Something urgent is taking place—an emergency. He and I need to leave immediately. I promise we'll talk, but not now."

"You also told me you wouldn't be here tonight. You lied to me."

A band tightened around his heart. It was more than that. He'd originally told her he'd escort her here. "My plans changed at the last minute. I didn't intentionally mislead you." But that was a lie too. He *had* tried to mislead her. He'd hoped she'd decide not to come to the Koliada Ball at all. Failing that, he'd hoped to be gone, his mission complete, before she arrived.

She looked doubtful.

"Please, Josephine. Go now. I must leave immediately. My business is urgent."

She narrowed her eyes, and something seemed to shift in her gaze. She looked more focused. More determined. "On one condition."

"What's that?"

She moved closer, slid her hands up his chest, wrapped them around his neck, and rose to her toes. "I need to remind you of something."

As she pressed her lips to his, she sent a tremor of desire coursing through him. She slid her fingers up the nape of his neck and into his hair, scraping her nails against his scalp in exactly the way he loved.

For a moment, he forgot the pain in his hands, his brother, his mission. All that mattered was the woman clinging to him. He could lose himself in her forever.

With a sigh, he slid his arms around her, and then his sigh turned into a gasp of pain.

Josephine stumbled back. "Did I hurt you?"

"No. It was my own fault. I forgot I was injured."

"See? The vodka worked."

"It wasn't the vodka," he said, his voice rasping and gruff. It was her. "You need to go."

She let out a small sigh. "Fine. I'll leave. I hope my reminder has left you with something to ponder." She gave him a saucy grin and swept out into the hallway, causing her hoop-skirt to swirl and sway around her in an alluring way.

He followed her to the entrance. A noise came from somewhere down the hallway—a door opening? When he glanced toward it, he saw nothing. He turned back to watch as Josephine opened the concealed door leading to the servants' staircase and disappeared through it, closing it with a whisper of sound.

Frederick backed into the bedroom and shut the door behind him. Carefully, he wiped down the tumbler he'd just used, hiding any sign they'd been there. He gathered up the sodden cloth. He even tucked the spent matchstick into his coat pocket. He glanced around the room one last time and then bent to blow out the light.

He needed to find his brother now. Did it really take Robert this long to pick a lock and snatch a book?

Josephine hurried back toward the ballroom. As she entered the foyer, she spotted a petite woman in a silver ball gown coming down the grand staircase. Had she been upstairs as well? She and Frederick must have narrowly missed being discovered.

The silver-gowned woman spoke to the footman, who whirled around, startled to see her. While his back was turned, Josephine darted past them. The footman appeared angry, and she didn't want him to turn his furious gaze on her.

The children's choir had completed their performance, and now the members of the orchestra were tuning their instruments. Dancing would resume shortly, although with this oppressive heat, many people might choose not to exert themselves.

Someone had opened the doors leading to the rear of the embassy, and the cool winter breeze was a blessing. She caught sight of a refreshment table and suddenly realized she was famished.

She filled a plate with some delicious-looking items. After a brief search, she found a quiet spot near a piano in one of the salons and settled in to ponder her next steps.

Perhaps that was her problem. She pondered too much. Sometimes action was required, not rumination.

She bit into a meat-filled dumpling as she considered what had just transpired upstairs. She shouldn't have let Frederick send her away. Instead, she should have followed through on her plan to confront him. But, no, she'd allowed her sympathy for him to alter her plans. Those burns. She shuddered. He must be in a world of pain.

Had she lost her best and only chance to demand an explanation? When would she find a better opportunity to be alone with him? He'd certainly done an admirable job of avoiding her all week. She tried something that looked like a thin pancake with caviar on top. Quite good. Perhaps she'd take some more.

At least fifteen minutes had passed since she'd come downstairs. Frederick must have left already to deal with his urgent matter. She wouldn't see him again tonight. So when would she see him again? With the burns he'd suffered, it was unlikely he'd be attending any social events in the next few days.

Fiddlesticks. She nibbled at an interesting mushroom concoction. Delicious.

Her plate was empty now. She glanced around. She should mingle rather than simply remain standing here. She'd abandoned Tristan, poor man. He deserved an apology.

A glimmer of silvery fabric caught her eye. There went that same silver-gowned woman again—the one she'd seen descending the stairs—and now she appeared to be hurrying toward the cloakroom. Was she leaving? So early? Josephine watched her departure longingly, wondering if she could follow suit.

Her sudden urge to leave surprised her. She normally enjoyed events such as these, but she now realized she didn't want to stay here. In fact, she didn't *have* to.

She could go. No one held dominion over her. She was her own woman. She could leave if she wanted to.

And she would.

With that decided, she spun around and came face to face with Frederick. Even as she let out a gasp of surprise, she reached out and touched his arm, pulling him to a halt.

"Josephine—I mean, Lady Harrington." Frederick's face reddened.

She yanked her hand away. "'Lady Harrington'?" Not Josephine? His use of her title felt like a public rejection. "We're back to that?" At least her voice sounded cool and firm. She'd been afraid it would crack from the tension. What was he even doing here? "I'm surprised to see you. I thought you needed to leave most urgently." Humiliation welled, threatening to spill over. "After the way you hurried me downstairs with claims of a life-or-death emergency, I never dreamed you'd still be here." She shot Lord Wentworth a significant glance. "I see nothing dreadful befell your brother." She lifted her chin, daring him to tell the truth. Daring him to appease her.

Frederick simply stared at her, not uttering a word. He didn't even try to defend himself. He'd lied to her again, and he knew he was well and truly caught.

Lord Wentworth turned away, obviously embarrassed by witnessing their confrontation.

She was so angry with Frederick right now that it was a struggle to hold her tongue. She pressed her lips firmly together. She had a great deal she wanted to say to Mr. Woolsy, but none of it was suited to their current surroundings.

Just then, a man pushed past them and jostled Frederick, causing him to let out a hiss of pain.

"Pardon me," the man said, not even pausing.

Frederick's face seemed to grow even paler as he clenched his teeth.

Josephine loosened her grip on Frederick's sleeve and glanced down at his hand, noting the cloth she'd wrapped around it. How could she have forgotten his injuries so quickly? "Are you in much pain?"

Frederick gave a stiff shrug and glanced away. "The vodka helped."

"He puts on a brave front," his brother said, "but I think we should leave and tend to his injury."

"Then I'll go with you." Now that she'd found Frederick again, she wasn't letting him get away. Not until she'd had the chance to speak with him privately. "My housekeeper is quite skilled at concocting poultices. I'll send for her. She can meet us at your home." She forced a false, polite smile. "That will allow us to have that conversation you've been avoiding."

When Frederick shot his brother a pleading look, a stab of pain and humiliation pierced her. She hid her reaction, not wanting him to see the hurt he caused her. Was the prospect of speaking with her so onerous?

"That isn't necessary," Lord Wentworth said. "I'd hate to inconvenience you. Our physician can care for him."

"Fiddlesticks. I couldn't possibly stay and enjoy myself knowing that Fre—Mr. Woolsy is suffering." She pressed her lips in a thin line. She hated this pretense of formality, but it felt as though Frederick had imposed it upon her when he'd used her title. After being on such intimate terms with him, this forced decorum galled her.

"I can assure you, Lady Harrington, there's no need for you to trouble yourself." Frederick glared at Lord Wentworth. "My brother is using my hand as an excuse for leaving when the true reason lies with him. Don't abandon the ball on my account."

Frederick's sudden flare of anger startled her. "I beg to disagree," she said. "I examined your hand earlier and am well aware of the severity of the burn." She peered at him more closely, and she didn't like what she saw. "You're quite pale and there is a sheen about you I find most troubling. I believe your hand pains you much more than you're willing to admit."

At that, Lord Wentworth also peered at Frederick. He frowned. "Perhaps we should accept her offer."

"We?" Frederick's voice was sharp with irritation as he spun to glare at his brother. "I was unaware that you'd been burned as well."

"It's settled." Lord Wentworth's tone was firm as he ignored Frederick's sharp comment and gestured toward the cloakroom.

"No, it isn't," Frederick said too loudly.

Josephine spotted the flutter of his pulse as it pounded rapidly in his throat. This must have been what Frederick meant earlier when he'd said he became irritable when he drank. No wonder he preferred to avoid alcohol.

"Not here. Not now," Lord Wentworth said. "Don't compound tonight's mistakes by drawing attention to us."

Her eyes darted from one brother to the other as she became even more confused. Why were they behaving so strangely? First Frederick had informed her he wouldn't escort her here, saying he'd stay home tonight, and then he'd appeared, only to avoid her and sneak upstairs. Now his brother was obviously concerned about drawing unwanted attention. None of it made sense.

Unless—was Frederick on an assignment for the Queen? Had she stumbled upon one of his missions?

Frederick glared at his brother. "My biggest mistake was relying on you. Tonight has been an unmitigated catastrophe."

Lord Wentworth's spine stiffened. "I already apologized for my error and I'm trying to correct it, but I'm not the only one who made mistakes tonight."

"Fine," Frederick said too loudly, "have it your way. *Eto moya vina.*"

When Josephine noticed the startled glances the nearby guests sent their way, she flushed with embarrassment. Now they *were* drawing attention. Quite a lot of it.

As he glanced around, Lord Wentworth seemed to take in the censorious glares focused on them. He stepped closer to his brother, lowered his voice, and in a crisp tone said, "Rather than staging a public scene, I suggest we call for our carriage."

Josephine nodded, lending him her enthusiastic support.

"Fine," Frederick snapped, "but I refuse to rely on you again. I'll call for the carriage myself." He spun on his heel and stalked in the direction of the cloakroom.

What on earth? This was so unlike Frederick. Josephine stared at his back as he stalked away. She glanced at Lord Wentworth, raising her eyebrows in surprise, but he simply shrugged. "The injury's making him short-tempered."

There was more to it, of that she was certain, but this wasn't the place to discuss what had just transpired. Instead, she nodded and took off after Frederick.

As she reached his side, she heard him instructing a footman to call for the carriage. Being careful not to aggravate his burns, he cautiously shrugged into his coat while the woman in the cloakroom helped Josephine don her cloak. Josephine took a moment use a pencil and a scrap of paper the attendant handed her to scribble a note to her housekeeper.

When Josephine glanced across the room, she spied Lord Wentworth speaking with Ambassador Revnik. She tensed. The ambassador seemed to be gesturing toward her and Frederick.

She gave Frederick an assessing gaze, taking in his pallor. He didn't look well. Not at all. Perhaps a bit of conversation would distract him. It certainly couldn't hurt. "You spoke in Russian earlier, didn't you? What did that mean?"

Frederick looked at her blankly as he clumsily tugged his top hat onto his head using his left hand.

"You spoke to your brother. '*Eto moya*' something..."

His eyes cleared for a moment as he focused on her. "*Eto moya vina*. It's all my fault," he translated. His face was glum as he shook his head. "The entire evening's been a disaster."

"I didn't know you spoke Russian."

"No?" His face softened for an instant as a smile flickered at the edges of his mouth and then disappeared. "I'm afraid there's a great deal you don't know about me."

She bit back a retort. This wasn't the time or the place to reveal everything she knew about him. Instead, she offered a sweet smile. "Do you speak any other languages?"

"French, of course. Italian. Spanish. I'm currently learning Turkish."

Her eyes widened. She'd always wanted to visit Constantinople, and they spoke Turkish there. A challenging language, indeed. "Turkish would be helpful." And then she shot him a mischievous grin. "I knew you had a talented tongue."

His eyes darkened and deepened as he seemed to recall exactly what he'd done with his tongue to earn her praise. He glanced down at her mouth, swaying toward her in a movement that was both infinitesimal and undeniable. He wanted her, she was certain of it.

Then why had he been avoiding her all week?

She moved closer to bridge the gap separating them, but he shifted back, maintaining his distance. Josephine let out an inaudible huff of frustration. The man was baffling.

A footman announced their carriage was ready just as Lord Wentworth joined them. She quietly directed the footman to call for her carriage and then handed him a note. "Give this to my coachman and instruct him to deliver it to my housekeeper immediately."

Frederick ushered her out the door and into the cold night. A number of stable boys and footmen huddled in a tight clump, probably for warmth. One broke away and hurried over to escort them to their carriage.

Lord Wentworth stepped to one side and leaned on a slim black cane as the footman opened the carriage door. Frederick moved in front of the young footman and lifted his hand to assist Josephine into the carriage. She glanced at the loose bandages covering his burns and then carefully placed her hand on his forearm rather than risk injuring him further. She slid to the far end of the seat in the carriage, and he settled into the spot next to her.

"Thank you, Frederick," she said softly.

She noted a faint blush suffuse his cheeks.

"Why did you revert to calling me Lady Harrington? I much prefer it when you call me Josephine."

"I'd intended to protect your reputation," Frederick said, looking faintly embarrassed, "but you seem firmly committed to tarnishing it. Nearly everyone at the ball saw you leave with me."

"Fiddlesticks. A widow has much more latitude than a débutante."

"Not this much."

Was he truly worried about what people thought of her? His concern was sweet, but misguided. "Your brother is with us, and neither of you is rumored to be a rake. My reputation is safe enough."

As Lord Wentworth climbed into the carriage, she glanced at him. "You should call me Josephine as well."

"Thank you. You must call me Robert." He claimed the seat opposite them. "It's quite kind of you to offer your assistance, Josephine."

She smiled at his use of her name.

"She didn't offer. She insisted." Frederick turned to frown at her.

"Fiddlesticks. This will be more expedient. My coachman can collect my housekeeper and bring her to you. You wouldn't want me sitting outside in the cold waiting for her, would you?"

Frederick's expression softened. "Of course not."

They sat in an awkward silence for a moment. At least, it was awkward for her. The brothers seemed comfortable with it. She tried to sit there quietly, truly she did, but it wasn't in her nature.

"Robert, what did the ambassador want?" she finally asked, breaking the silence. "He seemed quite intent on speaking with you."

Robert glanced at Frederick. "Nothing in particular," he murmured.

That was no answer. It was an evasion, and she'd had enough of men withholding information from her. She had the feeling Frederick had been doing it all night. She narrowed her eyes at Robert. "He seemed insistent."

The corners of Robert's mouth tensed. "He witnessed our argument and came over to investigate."

"Were you able to explain everything to his satisfaction?" Frederick asked, his tone sharp.

"I mentioned I'd eaten a bad shrimp and had an urgent need to return home. It turned out he already knew about my pretended illness, which I found peculiar." The brothers shared a glance that seemed full of hidden meaning. "He assumed you were in a temper because of your burned hand."

Josephine was appalled. Had the ambassador actually used those words? "'In a temper'?" she repeated. "Is that how he characterizes a man who is injured during his ball?" Anything that happened to a guest was ultimately his responsibility, including an intoxicated guest who set people on fire. If she had the ambassador in front of her right now, she'd show him exactly what it looked like when someone was in a temper.

"That's the proper term to use when anyone lets their anger take control of them in a public setting," Robert replied, his voice calm.

"You're one to talk," Frederick muttered. "I can't count the number of times I've seen you lose your temper."

Robert ignored the comment. "We need a plan."

Frederick inhaled and held his breath for a moment. Josephine had the impression he was attempting to regain his equilibrium after his flash of annoyance. Frederick met his brother's gaze with a level one. "I assumed you'd prefer to be quit of me and tonight's entanglements. I know how much you dislike being involved in my work."

"Unfortunately, I have the disadvantage of being responsible for" —he glanced at her, obviously not wanting to speak openly— "for what went wrong. I'm already involved, and I plan to rectify my error."

More secrets. She found herself mired in them tonight.

"Hmm," Frederick replied, sounding more annoyed than convinced. "In that case, it would be best for you to focus on recalling where you've seen your thief before. I think we should separate and pursue this problem from different angles. You go after the girl while I focus on the people I believe are behind the" —he glanced at Josephine—"the incident."

Something snapped inside her. She'd had enough. He'd heaped lies upon evasions, and now he wanted to go charging off into the night to chase down some thief, burns and all. "You should be resting," she said in sharp, clipped tones.

Frederick let out a sigh. "Josephine, more is taking place tonight than is apparent. If you'll refrain from asking questions for the moment, I'll do my best to explain everything later."

"Of course 'more is taking place,'" she snapped. Honestly, did he think her such a fool? She shifted in her seat to face him. "I assume it has something to do with your work for the Foreign Office. Is that why you were at the embassy tonight? To spy on the Russians?"

When Frederick's jaw dropped, she let a slow smile spread across her face. She'd genuinely surprised him. What a delicious feeling. "Don't worry, darling. I'll never repeat a word. I'm completely discreet."

"How—how long have you known?" Frederick asked.

"Oh, my. It's been quite some time now." She tapped her gloved index finger against her lower lip. "At least a year. Perhaps a bit more."

Frederick looked astounded. "And you never confronted me?"

"I didn't want to intrude," she said, holding up her palms in a gesture of denial. "I assumed you'd tell me eventually, but since tonight's situation appears to be a pressing one, I decided to reveal what I know." She dropped her hands to her lap as she gave Robert a sympathetic look. "I'm guessing the two of you were forced to improvise after Lord Percival's fire. That must have been a challenge."

Frederick let out an exasperated sigh. "If you knew all of that, why did you follow me upstairs?"

"I *am* sorry about that. I didn't realize you must have been on an assignment until later. I'd make a terrible spy, wouldn't I? I never considered that I might one day stumble across you while you were on a mission. I always imagined those sorts of tasks taking place in dark, scurrilous places."

Frederick held his palm out, gesturing for her to stop. "I really must speak candidly with my brother. I'd rather not involve you in this any further. It's safer for you if you don't know anything. We'll halt the carriage so he and I can walk for a moment."

"Fiddlesticks," she said, affronted. "I'd never betray you. I never said a word about what happened last year with Lord and Lady Huntley, did I? And I never will. Nor will I repeat anything you say in front of me now. Pretend I'm not here."

Frederick remained silent.

"You already trust her," Robert said, "otherwise she wouldn't be in the carriage with us right now. You'd never have permitted it."

Josephine felt a rush of gratitude, but she kept her attention focused on Frederick.

He met Josephine's gaze. "Trust isn't the issue," he said, stroking the back of his left hand against her cloak. That faint, tenuous connection shot a spear of awareness through her chest. "I want to protect you from this part of my life, not drag you into it. But you're right. I've already involved you in this. Too many people saw us leave together."

She took a steadying breath, but whether her need for something solid to cling to was driven by his words or his touch, she couldn't have said. "I can take care of myself," she insisted. "I've been doing so for the past two years."

Frederick's jaw tensed, but after a long pause, he nodded. "Letting you listen won't put you at any greater risk."

Josephine listened as the brothers discussed what had transpired that evening. Listened, but didn't interrupt. Their objective tonight seemed to have been to acquire a book. A church register, of all things. Apparently the French, the Russians, and the Ottomans wanted it as well. From what she could gather, Frederick and Robert needed to recover it from some unknown woman who had managed to steal it from them before escaping from the embassy.

What sort of woman was she? She must be a spy. A woman spy. And a skilled one at that. She must be if she could blend in at an embassy ball, fool Robert into letting down his guard, and slip away with the prize. Certainly she was clever, resourceful, and determined. But so was Frederick. So who was the thief working for? Obviously not the British.

Frederick let out a deep sigh. "If I'm right and the French are behind the theft, I might be able to deduce the identity of the man who orchestrated tonight's debacle. You mentioned the thief had a key. There aren't many people who would have been able to acquire one. Nor are there many people with the skills and connections to have choreographed tonight's events. Your little thief will probably pass along the church register as soon as possible. Once I've deduced his identity, I can watch him until she shows herself. As soon as she makes contact, I'll grab the book."

Robert nodded. "It's a solid plan, as long as you're certain you know who her contact will be."

"That's the problem. This is my best guess, but since I'm missing key facts, I could be wrong. That's why I want you to try to locate the woman using your own methods. If we attack the problem from two different directions, we have a better chance of succeeding."

Josephine began shaking her head vehemently. "I don't like this. I know I promised that you wouldn't know I was here, but I can't remain silent. You're injured, you're tired, and you've been drinking. You shouldn't go haring off alone in the dark after some thief."

"I have no choice. You don't understand the severity of the situation. It is imperative that we recover that book. Everything depends upon it."

"Not without my help," Josephine insisted. When Frederick opened his mouth to protest, she held up her hand to silence him and continued speaking. "I'll accompany you. I refuse to allow you to do this alone. It's obvious your brother needs to be elsewhere, so I'm the only person who can help you."

"I like the plan," Robert said, surprising her. "The book is too important to allow anything to get in the way. Recovering it has to be our priority."

"I know this will come as a surprise to both of you, but I like the plan too," Frederick said.

A surge of relief washed through her. "Thank goodness," she murmured.

As Frederick went over some details with Robert, Josephine made her own plans. Frederick really shouldn't go out again. Once he was home, she'd convince him to take better care of himself and retire for the evening. He needed to rest. And if she couldn't sway him with logic, she'd do her best to soothe him into compliance. Pampering had a way of lowering a man's defenses and making him more amenable to suggestions. She knew what was best for him, even if he didn't.

Just past Hyde Park, Robert banged his cane on the ceiling of the carriage, causing Josephine to jump in fright. He must have done it to get his coachman's attention, because the carriage pulled to an abrupt halt.

"What are you doing?" Frederick asked.

"There's no need for me to return home with you. I need to remember where I saw that woman, and I'll think better if I'm walking."

$\maltese$ 3 $\maltese$

Frederick suppressed his sigh of relief as the carriage pulled up to the entrance of Woolsy House. The tension between him and Josephine had begun to build with his brother's abrupt departure, but he'd managed to resist breaking the silence. He didn't want to confront Josephine—not when he felt so miserable and she looked so confident. If she pressed him now, all his secrets would come spilling out, and that could only hurt her. He'd lied to her so many times, he'd lost count. What kind of man treated a woman he cared for in such a disrespectful manner? Only someone callous could be so manipulative.

That was him. Callous and manipulative. Not at all a suitable match for a woman as vibrant and glorious as Josephine. That much was clear.

His one solace was that he only lied to protect her, both from the dangers of his life and from the stress and anxiety the truth would bring her. After all, what good would the truth do? None that he could see. She'd only worry about him. Be fearful every time he left for a mission. Truth would cause her pain, and he'd do anything to protect her, even from him.

Frederick hurried to exit the carriage, avoiding touching the door frame with his injured hand and instead jumping to the pavement.

As he turned back to face the carriage, Josephine appeared in the open doorway, looking radiant with her glossy blond hair peeking out from beneath the hood of her celadon-blue cloak. He froze for a moment at the sight. Her skin was pale in the moonlight. Her blue eyes with their thick blond lashes caught the reflected light of the lamps flanking his front door, and the flames made them shift and flicker with secrets of her own.

This wasn't the first time he'd wondered at Josephine's depths. She presented a smooth, cool demeanor to the world, but at times she allowed him glimpses of her inner self—the woman who lived within that beautiful exterior.

He shook off the moment of bemusement and moved closer to offer her his arm to help her descend safely. She placed her hand on his forearm near his elbow in an obvious attempt to avoid touching his burns, just as she'd done back at the embassy.

As they climbed the steps leading to his front door, it swung open. Landon, his butler, stood at the entrance.

A wave of relief surged through him as he entered his home, taking him by surprise. He held Josephine a bit more tightly for a moment, unaccountably pleased to have her here.

"Good evening, sir," Landon said, "and good evening, Lady Harrington." His normally impassive face suddenly betrayed him as his assessing butler's glance landed on Frederick's bandaged hands. His eyes widened in surprise.

"My housekeeper will be arriving shortly," Josephine said. "She's bringing materials to make a poultice for Frederick's burns,. Please send her to the drawing room when she arrives."

"Yes, my lady," Landon replied. "Shall I bring some ice while you wait?" At Frederick's raised eyebrow, the butler cleared his throat. "In my experience, the cold from the ice draws out the heat from the burns. It should alleviate some of your pain."

Frederick gave a shrug. "Bring it." The bundle of ice he'd held at the Russian embassy had helped. He was more than willing to try it again. With Landon's assistance, he slid out of his coat and managed not to brush the sleeves against his burns.

He glanced at Josephine as she shed her cloak, arching her back in the process. The scooped neckline of her gown and her lustrous pearl necklace drew his attention to her perfectly rounded breasts as they momentarily pressed toward him. The stunning sight made his mouth go dry.

Frederick whipped around and strode toward the drawing room without waiting for Landon's reply. He knew he was behaving rudely by walking away from Josephine so abruptly, but he needed to distance himself from her, if only briefly. She followed him as he entered the room, but she stayed far enough away for him to regain his composure.

Ruthlessly, he turned his thoughts back to the book—back to his duty. Tonight had been a disaster. These next few hours would be crucial if he had any hope of recovering from it.

His hands throbbed with pain as the effects of the vodka wore off. Perhaps he should take another drink—but no. He needed to keep his wits about him. Pain might slow his thinking process, but alcohol would be much worse.

A moment later, Landon entered the room carrying a large container of ice. He spread out a small towel as he began preparing to assemble a bundle of ice, but Josephine shooed him away. "I'd prefer to do that," she said. "Can you wait for my house-keeper and bring her here as soon as she arrives?"

Landon gave a stiff nod and left the room. Josephine turned her attention to vigorously attacking the small block of ice with the ice pick, breaking it into smaller chunks. Watching her breasts bob with her effort had a mesmerizing effect on Frederick.

"Here," she said a few glorious moments later, turning toward him and handing him the bundle of ice chips. "Sit for a moment and let the ice numb some of the pain. I'll pour you another drink."

"No more spirits," he said, swallowing as he accepted the bundle. He dropped heavily onto the garnet-colored sofa. "You know, you don't need to take care of me. Landon is quite capable of doing so." Frederick pressed the cloth to his hand and almost sighed with relief as he felt the cold seep into his fingertips. "Although I must admit, you are a much more pleasant companion than he is. Much more attractive too."

She blushed and turned her back on him, busying herself with wiping away some flakes of ice that had fallen on the side table. "Thank you," she said without turning around. "I'd begun to wonder if my presence here was more of an irritation than a balm."

Frederick shook his head decisively, but since her back was to him, she couldn't see him. "I doubt you could ever irritate me even if you put your mind to it," he said. His voice sounded gruff, so he tried to even it out. "Quite the contrary. I find your presence unaccountably soothing." He hadn't been able to eliminate the emotion from his tone, but at least he didn't sound angry any longer.

She turned to face him. Her head was dipped slightly as she peered at him. She seemed to be trying to gauge his mood. She seemed to like what she saw, because a slow, sultry smile began to spread over her lips as she took a step closer to him.

Something banged at the door of the drawing room, startling them both. Frederick was stunned when the door flew open and an older woman came bustling in, carrying a bag.

Josephine's jaw dropped at the sight as well, but her expression of surprise was quickly replaced by one of pleased satisfaction.

Their unexpected guest wore a dark-green coat buttoned askew. Her mulberry-colored hat sat at a worrisome angle, looking as though it would fall to the floor at any moment. The entire ensemble gave her a decidedly lopsided appearance that wasn't helped by the large and obviously heavy basket looped over one arm.

"This is my housekeeper, Mrs. Drummer," Josephine announced. "A more versatile woman you'll never find. She's extremely knowledgeable regarding herbal remedies. I think you'll be quite pleased."

Before Frederick could rise to greet her, the woman hurried across the room and claimed the seat next to him on the sofa. She plunked her large basket on the floor by her feet. "May I see?" Mrs. Drummer asked, holding out her hands and glancing toward his.

With one last dubious glance at her hat, he held them out. "I hope you can help. As fate would have it, tonight has been a complete disaster."

"No one can ever predict what the three Moirai have planned for us," Josephine said.

Mrs. Drummer gently stripped away the damp bandages and then cradled his hands while she examined them. She clucked her tongue in dismay. "My, but those look painful." She shot him a smile full of reassurance. "Don't worry, I'll have you feeling better in no time."

"The Moirai? They're from Greek mythology, right?" He searched his memory. "Weren't they the three Fates?" Frederick asked. "Do you believe in that sort of thing?"

"That our lives are predetermined?" The corner of her mouth turned up. "That concept doesn't fit into my philosophy of life. I believe our choices drive our outcomes, not merely some external force."

Frederick sat up a bit straighter. "Are you saying it's a combination of the two? Both self-determination and fate?"

Mrs. Drummer stood and picked up her basket before crossing to a nearby desk. She opened the basket's hinged wooden lid, peered inside it, and extracted a cloth bag along with a mortar and pestle. She commenced pulling out handfuls of fresh green leaves from the cloth bag and tossing them into the bowl. She tore them into smaller pieces and then began to smash them together using the pestle. The pungent smell of the broken leaves drifted toward him. It wasn't unpleasant—very fresh in fact. Then she splashed a bit of liquid into the bowl and mixed it all a bit longer.

"I think the circumstances of our birth wield the greatest influence on our lives. I'll never be queen because I wasn't born to it, nor will I be the captain of one of Her Majesty's warships since I'm not a man. Even so, that doesn't mean I can't exert control over my own life through the choices I make. I choose my friends. The foods I eat. The places I go. No one else controls these things." She drew closer to observe Mrs. Drummer's preparations. "But then again, I'm fortunate in this. Most of my friends don't have my level of freedom. Their husbands make those choices for them."

Mrs. Drummer extracted a length of flannel from the bag, pulled a pair of scissors from her pocket, cut off a strip of fabric, and then spread the mashed leaves over it.

"Did Lord Harrington treat you that way? Did he limit your choices?"

She tensed. "More so than I would have liked." She shook her head, glancing at Mrs. Drummer as though trying to decide how much she wanted to reveal in her presence. "I'd thought we'd travel around the world once we'd married. I've always wanted to visit Anatolia, Greece, Rome, so many places. He promised we'd go, but he never made it a priority, despite his promises. My husband was a good man—just—"

"Just a bit too thoughtless and overbearing?" Frederick suggested.

"Perhaps a bit. He meant well, but he had the need to be in control of everything. I found it wearing at times."

"This should help," Mrs. Drummer said, carrying her concoction toward Frederick. He glanced at it. The poultice didn't look like much of anything at all. Just a thick green mess.

Mrs. Drummer sat next to him. "Give me your bad hand," she said.

Frederick glanced at the clock above the fireplace mantel. Nearly twenty minutes had passed since he'd entered this room. He could sense the church register slipping farther and farther away with each passing second.

He held out his right hand. She cradled it as she gently draped the poultice across his burns. The light pressure of the flannel hurt at first, but at least the leaves were cool. A moment later, however, the poultice began to take effect. The pain receded quickly. It didn't disappear entirely, but it was no longer all-consuming.

The moment the pain eased its grip on him, Frederick began to think more clearly. He hadn't realized how much energy he'd been expending on suppressing it, but now that his mind was crisp and sharp once again, he found himself immediately focusing on finding the book.

The identity of the person who'd orchestrated tonight's theft suddenly came to him, as crisp and clear as if the man were standing before him. It had to have been the Frenchman— Monsieur LeCompte. The fact that the thief possessed a key had troubled Frederick. It was a clue. An enormous one. Not even Frederick had managed to obtain a key.

Only LeCompte possessed the requisite skills to set tonight's events in motion. The embassy's renovations had only recently been completed, and LeCompte was one of the few people who could have acquired a key to the new locks. He was also one of the few who could have procured an invitation to the ball for the mysterious thief. Those two facts placed him on a very short list of suspects. What made him stand out was the fact that he possessed a strong motivation to acquire the book, a motivation that was nearly identical to Frederick's. LeCompte wanted

Emperor Napoleon to be able to use it as leverage against Czar Nicholas.

An intense sense of urgency swept over Frederick. Time was of the essence. His duty couldn't wait—not for an evening, not even for another hour. He knew what his country demanded of him. He had to send Josephine away from here as quickly as possible, and he had to locate the Frenchman and retrieve the church register.

Frederick barely contained his impatience as Mrs. Drummer used strips of linen to wrap the poultice in place on his right hand. Then she began treating his other hand.

When Frederick glanced at Josephine, his mental resolve weakened. She was beautiful tonight. She'd swept her glossy blond hair up into a chignon, and gossamer tendrils framed her face.

She met his gaze, but hers was full of concern. For him.

Her sweet mouth with its slightly fuller lower lip was tense with worry. This was only one of the many expressions her eloquent face had presented to him over the past few months. He'd seen those sweet lips drawn up in a bow of delight or tightened in a frown of consternation. Only a week ago he'd seen them swollen and ripe with his kisses, and he'd love nothing more than to see them that way again. Tonight.

But, no, not tonight. He needed to send her away, and to do that, he needed to persuade her it was for the best.

As he observed her, he realized her definition of what was "for the best" would be quite different from his. Her priority would be to care for him and promote his recovery, while his was to track down LeCompte and retrieve that book. How would he convince her that his mission needed to take precedence over his well-being?

The realization came crashing down on him. It came down to choices again. And his were limited. If he wanted to leave quickly, he'd need to lie to her. To control and manipulate her.

The thought galled him, even as he steeled himself to do it.

How had he come to this? How had he turned into the sort of man who manipulated and lied to someone he cared for?

"Is the poultice helping?" Josephine asked.

The hopeful look on her face pierced him. He didn't deserve her sympathy. He realized this even as he nodded. Even as he began lying to her. "The pain has eased considerably." He faked a broad yawn. "Pardon me. It appears the night's events took more of a toll than I'd realized."

"You need to rest. I'm certain you'll feel much better in the morning."

Mrs. Drummer shook her head. "By morning, the effects of the poultice will have disappeared and you'll need to reapply it. Lady Harrington is right though. You should catch whatever rest you can now while the pain is at bay. It's unlikely you'll sleep through the night."

He let his eyelids droop slightly. "In that case, perhaps I should retire now."

"Yes. I believe that's just the thing." A broad smile of approval lit up Josephine's face, and it made him feel like a manipulative cad.

He was a scoundrel. An unmitigated scoundrel.

"Mrs. Drummer and I will leave you to recuperate," Josephine said.

The housekeeper gestured toward the bag on the table. "I'll leave these supplies so your valet can prepare a fresh poultice once this one begins to lose its potency." She quickly rattled off instructions for making it. Frederick listened closely and committed the steps to memory.

He rose to his feet as Mrs. Drummer collected her basket. It was obviously much lighter, but when she looped it over her arm, she still appeared lopsided. That was probably because she'd never addressed the problem with her misaligned buttons.

Josephine eased closer to him. "I'm glad we were able to help you."

"Thank you for your thoughtfulness. I don't deserve it," he said. Josephine looked enormously pleased by this, and her smile skewered his lying heart, forcing him to look away.

Tonight's lies were for England. For the Queen. At least, he tried to tell himself that. Unfortunately, it did nothing to ease his guilt.

Shouldn't he at least be truthful to himself? Tonight's lies hadn't been simply to protect her. They'd been to manipulate her into behaving a certain way. The lie had been more expedient than the truth, and that self-knowledge left him feeling raw.

Apparently he now lied simply because it was convenient. He'd sunk even lower than he'd realized.

4

As Josephine stepped out the front door of Woolsy House, the cold night air slid its fingers around her, driving the warmth from her body. It hadn't seemed so cold when she'd first entered the house. Had the temperature dropped while she'd been ensconced with Frederick, or had his presence earlier kept the chill at bay?

Her coachman stepped forward to escort her to her carriage. "Where would you like me to take you, m'lady?" he asked as he opened her carriage door.

Despite wanting to hurry into the carriage, she paused and stared into its dim interior as she considered the question. Should she return to the Koliada Ball? She glanced back at the front door of Woolsy House. She dreaded the thought of returning to the Russian ambassador's stuffy, overheated ballroom, but her quiet home didn't appeal to her either. Unfortunately, she couldn't think of anyplace else she wanted to go at this time of the night. Not alone. She let out a heavy sigh. "Home," she said.

As she settled inside the carriage, her thoughts drifted to the book currently sitting on the table next to her bed, and she gave a slight smile. She'd been looking forward to reading more about the tomb Mr. Fellows had discovered in Lycia, and tonight would offer her the perfect opportunity. Charles Fellows had discovered what appeared to be a Greek tomb in Anatolia—a region that had never been a part of Greece. The elaborate and enormous structure was a mystery, one she found fascinating.

Josephine unfolded the traveling blanket from the seat next to her and draped it across both her lap and Mrs. Drummer's. The coachman handed each of them a hot brick wrapped in cloth. Josephine cupped her hands around hers on her lap, savoring its warmth.

She stared down at her gloved hands in the dim interior glow of the carriage lamp, but the image was immediately replaced by the memory of Frederick's fire-ravaged hands.

Tonight had been entirely unexpected, from beginning to end.

What was she to do about Frederick? He'd slowly and relentlessly pursued her for months, never giving up until he'd finally broken down her resistance and seduced his way into her bed and into her heart. He'd convinced her she was special. That she was important to him—

And then he'd ignored her.

Had his presence at the embassy ball truly been a last-minute decision, or had he simply lied to her? The mere fact that this was a question in her mind told her a great deal about their relationship.

Obviously, she didn't trust him.

He'd lied to her before, she was certain of it, but only to conceal his activities as a spy. At least, that's what she'd always believed.

Now she wasn't as certain. He might have been on a mission tonight, but that didn't explain why he'd avoided her all week.

"The burns on Mr. Woolsy's right hand were severe," Mrs. Drummer said as she placed her basket on the floor by their feet. "He'll recover, but I'll wager his sense of touch will be dulled for quite a few years."

"In both hands?" she asked, alarmed. Josephine wished she could make out Mrs. Drummer's features in the dim interior light of the carriage, but she could only see well enough to catch her movement as she shook her head.

"The ones on his left hand aren't as bad. He should recover well enough."

A coil of tension eased. "That's good news." She rubbed her fingers together, wondering what it would be like to lose the sensation of touch. She hoped it wouldn't hinder his work as a spy.

Being a spy meant everything to Frederick. It was his passion. She couldn't imagine separating the man from the role.

"I'm relieved to hear he plans to rest," Mrs. Drummer said. "He'll have a bad night of it. Those burns will keep him awake."

"I was worried he wouldn't see reason. Once he's chosen a course of action, he doesn't change his mind easily."

Mrs. Drummer nodded. "So he's one of those, is he? He had me fooled."

"One of those what?" Josephine peered at the woman's face in the darkness, but couldn't make out her expression.

"I've found injured men tend to fall into one of two broad categories. One group is chock full of men who are stubborn when it comes to their own healing. Their technique is to ignore the problem until it goes away on its own. I think it's because they hate to show any weakness. The other group—well, they're quite the opposite. They demand their due and expect everyone to cater to them, even when faced with a minor injury. Mr. Woolsy must be one of those rare men who doesn't fall into either category."

Josephine nodded. Her husband had been in that second category. She hadn't minded coddling him when he wasn't feeling well, but it would have been nice if he'd reciprocated when she'd been in a similar state. Instead, he'd avoided her when she was ill. He'd said he wanted her to rest and recuperate, but if so, why did he demand so much of her attention when he was unwell?

"At first I thought your Mr. Woolsy belonged in that first group, but I changed my mind when he turned into such a pussycat after I applied the poultice. Now I can't place him in either category."

"Is that so uncommon? I'd think anyone would be swayed to do as you say after they experience the effectiveness of your treatment."

"Men aren't nearly as logical as they'd like you to believe. Certainly not when they believe their masculinity is being threatened. Those stubborn ones tend to decide they were originally mistaken regarding the severity of the pain rather than admitting my poultice helped them. If you're right about how determined Mr. Woolsy is, his decision to stay home seems to go against character. Perhaps you hold more sway over him than you realize."

Josephine pulled at her glove, pleased to know she could encourage Frederick to behave responsibly regarding his health. Perhaps he truly did care for her.

Like errant children ignoring their mother's orders, Josephine's thoughts returned to Frederick's lie—the one in which he'd told her he couldn't attend tonight's ball. It worried her to know he'd deceived her so casually. So thoughtlessly. As though lying to her had become a reflex rather than a conscious decision.

Considering the nights they'd spent together, he should have been more solicitous toward her. Was it possible he didn't value her? The thought caused her stomach to tighten into a knot. She'd believed they had something more. Something real. Had she been fooling herself?

She tightened her grip on the cloth-wrapped brick. She wouldn't waste her time pining away for a man who didn't respect her. She refused to debase herself in such a way. Even if she managed to capture his attention, a man whose heart wasn't committed would quickly slip away. No, she firmly believed that a man she had to chase wasn't a man worth having. If he truly wanted her, he'd be the one to pursue her, not the other way around.

But Frederick *had* pursued her. Relentlessly. For an entire year.

Perhaps behavior earlier tonight had been an aberration. Perhaps he'd been telling her the truth about his last-minute change of plans. He'd also mentioned that alcohol had a strong effect on him. That, combined with his burns, might explain why he'd seemed so distant for much of the night.

The evening had ended so well. She'd enjoyed the time they'd spent alone together. She only wished it could have lasted longer. When he was open and honest with her, things were good between them. Tonight proved it.

Weighing her options, she finally decided to give Frederick one last chance. She'd drop off those poultice supplies in two days, speak with him, and then make a decision about their future together.

She hoped she wouldn't be forced to excise him from her life, but it would be better to do it now than to let his lies and her distrust poison their relationship.

Without trust, how could love flourish?

❦

THE MOMENT JOSEPHINE STEPPED OUT THE FRONT DOOR OF Woolsy House, Frederick sensed her absence. He'd felt it acutely all week, and seeing her tonight made him ache for her all the more. He'd have loved nothing more than to send away her housekeeper and keep Josephine with him all night long.

He let out a sigh. He wasn't fooling himself. He wanted to keep Josephine much longer than one night.

But that wasn't an option. She couldn't be his tonight. Perhaps not ever.

With a mental shake, he drove her from his thoughts and rang for Landon.

The butler appeared moments later. "I need to go out again," Frederick announced. He barely noticed his butler's grim-faced expression. The man so frequently disapproved of Frederick's actions that his face perpetually appeared as though he'd been sucking on a lemon. "Have the carriage brought around. Tell Turner he needs to accompany me. Instruct him to bring writing supplies."

"Yes, sir." Landon's voice held a droning quality that never quite revealed his opinion on any matter, but which always sounded disapproving. "I believe he retired for the evening, but I'm certain he can be ready to depart within ten minutes."

"That will do." The young footman Turner had proven adept as a spy's assistant. In fact, Frederick often wondered whether the young man might be of more help to England if he worked directly for the Foreign Office. He sometimes felt guilty keeping Turner in his employ as a footman, but—blast it—he'd be lost without the man's help. Of course, if Turner came to work for him in the Foreign Office—

That was an intriguing idea.

When Frederick glanced up, Landon still stood before him. "Was there something else?"

"I couldn't help but overhear you earlier, sir. You mentioned you were staying *in* for the evening." Landon glanced at Frederick's bandaged hands. "Has the poultice wrought some miracle?"

"Sarcasm, Landon? You astonish me." He shook his head. "I'll be fine. And to answer your question, yes, this poultice *has* been bloody well miraculous. Go fetch Turner, and be quick about it."

Landon was letting his tongue run away with him more and more often these days. That was the problem with having a butler who'd held the position since before Frederick had been born. He often behaved more like a family member than a servant.

Landon turned on his heel and strode out the door, his disapproval evident in each precise step, but at least he was doing as Frederick had directed.

A half hour later, Frederick and Turner sat side by side in Robert's carriage. They waited not far from Monsieur LeCompte's townhouse, and their vantage point offered a clear view of the front door. They both watched through LeCompte's brightly lit windows as he moved from room to room. He didn't appear to expect any guests, nor was he dressed to go out.

Perhaps Frederick had been wrong. Perhaps LeCompte wasn't the thief's accomplice. Or perhaps she'd already come and gone. Or perhaps LeCompte knew they were watching. Perhaps—perhaps—it was a perpetual guessing game. As he stared at the windows, Frederick evaluated the possibilities and developed a plan for each one.

Once he was satisfied with his mental preparations, Frederick let himself relax, if only a little. He still had work to do.

"I'm going to take a look around the area. Let me know if anyone comes to his house while I'm gone, anyone at all. Even if it's a deliveryman. If someone comes within ten feet of that door, I want to know."

"Yes, sir," Turner said.

"I'll only be gone for a few minutes, but if LeCompte leaves, you'll need to follow him to find out who he's meeting."

Turner's jaw flexed. "Yes, sir."

Frederick twisted the carriage door handle. His hand didn't hurt nearly as much as it had an hour ago. Mrs. Drummer was a miracle worker, and Josephine was a wondrous woman indeed to have sent for her.

As he stepped into the night, he recalled some of the more wondrous abilities she'd displayed only a week ago. If mere memories could keep him warm, these could do it.

FREDERICK RETURNED TO THE CARRIAGE AND SETTLED IN TO wait.

An hour or so later, Turner let out a hiss of warning. "LeCompte is preparing to leave."

Frederick opened his eyes with a start of surprise. He must have begun to doze off. Reflexively, he curled his hands into fists, causing them to sear with renewed pain. The poultice's powers were fading. The pain wasn't acute. Not yet. But it was definitely worsening.

He fought to become more alert. The cold had seeped into every part of his body, leaving him stiff and miserable. He sat up straight and clumsily rubbed his eyes using his thumb and forefinger, only to wince yet again at his own stupidity as pain blossomed in his hand.

"Good work." Frederick straightened himself in the seat and leaned forward to catch a glimpse of LeCompte through the window of the man's house. "We'll follow him. Let's see if he goes on foot or in a carriage." He analyzed the situation and quickly devised a plan. "I need you to wait in that alley and follow him on foot if necessary. If he gets in a carriage, hurry back and we'll follow him together."

As Turner opened the door and slipped outside, a chill gust of wind swept through the opening and drove away all remnants of fatigue still clinging to Frederick.

In the silence of the carriage, he kept his gaze pinned on the cobalt-blue rectangle of LeCompte's front door. Night nearly robbed the bright paint of its color, making it appear as dull and lackluster as the other doors on the street.

A hackney pulled to a stop in front of the house. Was a guest arriving, or had one of LeCompte's men sent for it? If so, he'd missed the servant's exit. What else might he have missed? A moment later, the front door of the townhouse opened, spilling warm yellow light across the bright blue door.

LeCompte stepped outside as he adjusted the thick scarf

around his neck against the chill. A young footman followed him. LeCompte paused and glanced up and down the street. LeCompte's gaze seemed to stop on Frederick's carriage for the briefest of moments, but then it moved on.

Had he been spotted? He held his breath, waiting to see what the Frenchman would do.

A moment later. LeCompte trotted down the steps toward the hackney. The game of fox and hound was about to commence.

LeCompte's footman snatched open the hackney's door just as LeCompte reached it and then ushered him into its depths.

The hackney immediately pulled away. Despite wanting to follow, Frederick waited as he stared into the darkness, searching for a sign of Turner. Where was the man? They needed to move quickly, before they lost LeCompte.

A dark figure darted toward him across the residential street. As it drew closer, Frederick recognized Turner. A moment later the entire conveyance bounced and swayed as the young man clambered up the side to sit with the driver. In an instant, the carriage took off with a jolt.

From inside the carriage, Frederick couldn't see LeCompte's hackney, but he trusted his coachman and footman to handle the pursuit.

A moment later, a small door in the carriage roof snapped open. Frederick glanced up and saw Turner's grinning face gazing down at him through the square frame, his excitement for the chase evident. "He took off quickly, but we managed to catch him," the young man announced.

"He might have seen the carriage. If so, he'll expect us to follow."

Turner's face bobbed up and down in the square. "We'll be careful."

The little door snapped shut, and Frederick could only smile at the young man's exuberance. On any other night, the two of them would be following LeCompte on horseback. He detested tracking someone at night while riding in a carriage, especially in one as distinctive as his. But the condition of his hands left him with little choice.

Was sitting inside the carriage the only reason his excitement for the chase had ebbed? He shifted restlessly. In truth, he resented that his duties had required that he set aside a much more enticing alternative.

Josephine.

Frederick let out a heavy sigh. What kind of life could he offer a woman? Especially someone like Josephine? A life of lies and missed engagements? A life of sitting home alone? Yes, she claimed to already know he was a spy, but that didn't mean she truly understood what that entailed. The sacrifices she'd be forced to make if she linked her life to his.

But his life was even more complicated than that of most spies. He harbored secrets within secrets. There was one in particular he was certain Josephine never would guess. A secret he and his brother had guarded for more than a decade. One secret that had shaped his childhood with its far-reaching consequences.

And it wasn't even *his* secret. It was his father's.

Josephine didn't know. No one knew, although a few might suspect.

Treason. His father had committed treason.

With his tragic and shortsighted decision, the late Lord Wentworth had launched his entire family on this fateful trajectory. Josephine was right about that. *Our decisions shape our destinies.* With every choice Frederick made since learning of his father's secret, he'd always taken it into consideration.

Every decision but for one. Being with Josephine.

His one weakness.

His one mistake.

He never should have pursued her. Never should have slipped into her bed. Not with this secret looming over him. Not with his father's treason casting a shadow over his future.

If he was lucky, no one would ever find out.

Unfortunately, he didn't believe in luck. Luck was for fools. A man made his own luck through hard work and attention to detail.

Eventually his father's secret would come to light. Someone would discover it. The only thing truly surprising was that it had remained hidden for so long.

Once that secret came out, Frederick's carefully constructed life would come crashing down, and anyone close to him would be brought down as well.

He couldn't do that to Josephine. He needed to keep her as far away from this as possible. He couldn't bear to have her tainted by this.

He'd break things off with her. There was no other choice.

A moment later, the carriage pulled to a halt. It shifted as someone climbed down, and a moment later the carriage door opened. Turner slipped inside.

"I'm sorry, Mr. Woolsy. It appears we've lost Monsieur LeCompte."

5

After a long and disappointing day of trying to track down the thief, Frederick was no closer to finding that book than he'd been the previous night.

He tapped his foot against the leg of a small side table in his bedroom as his valet, Herbert, finished re-bandaging his more severely injured hand. "These burns are a blasted nuisance," Frederick muttered. "It's only been a day and I'm already thoroughly sick of them." They'd caused him to sleep fitfully last night. Tonight probably wouldn't be any better.

Herbert shook his head as he scowled at the burns. "They're bad. Lord Percival owes you an apology." He smoothed more of the poultice directly onto Frederick's left hand, forgoing the bit of flannel. Fortunately, these burns were proving to be relatively insignificant. In fact, the blister along the outside of his littlest finger seemed to be smaller already. He'd only need a bit of poultice and a glove for his left hand.

Herbert held open an oversized glove and Frederick examined it, deciding the best angle at which to hold his hand while sliding it on.

"I doubt I'll get one," he said as he began slipping his hand inside. "In fact, he was so inebriated, I doubt he was aware he'd started the fire." He winced and pulled back as the blister on his smallest finger grazed a seam inside the glove. He adjusted the angle of his hand and tried again, this time successfully managing to sheath it.

He lifted his left hand and turned it from side to side. No one would be able to tell it had been burned. He'd even be able to use it if he was careful.

Unfortunately, his right hand was a different matter. Herbert generously swathed it in strips of cotton, but it still hurt like the blazes—or at least it *had* until Herbert had applied a freshly mixed batch of Mrs. Drummer's poultice to it. Frederick grimaced at the thick swaddling of bandages.

He viewed it as his own personal emblem of incompetence.

If not for the burns the bandages concealed, he wouldn't have been obliged to ask Robert for help, he wouldn't have been ambushed upstairs by Josephine, and the book wouldn't have been seduced away from his brother by that silver-gowned thief.

They'd come so close to success, only for it to be snatched away. Close really didn't matter. He'd lost the book. A book that might have averted a war.

Had Monsieur LeCompte spotted Frederick outside his home last night? He must have.

After the Frenchman left his house, they'd followed his hackney to its destination. When his carriage door opened and he'd emerged from its depths, they'd discovered the ruse. Another man had switched places with LeCompte—someone close to his size and wearing his clothes.

The impertinent rascal then yanked down his woolen scarf to reveal his face, tipped back his hat, and flashed Frederick a broad grin. He'd known they were following all along.

LeCompte, that trickster, had lured them into following the wrong hackney. Once he'd drawn them away, LeCompte must have rendezvoused with the thief. Frederick should have left Turner behind to watch things. Add that to his tally of missteps.

Herbert cleared his throat. Frederick glanced up. How long had Herbert been standing there holding Frederick's evening coat?

Frederick glanced at the mantel clock and then rose to his feet. Time to leave. He gingerly slid his right hand through the sleeve, being careful not to abrade the bandages. "I plan to meet with Lord Cary, so I'll probably be quite late."

"Yes, sir."

He had no idea how the spymaster would react to the news that he'd lost the church register. It was an enormous setback. Frederick had never before failed so abysmally at completing an assignment. It had been years since he'd needed to rely on Lord Cary's knowledge and resources to help him untangle a tricky problem.

Fortunately, Lord Cary enjoyed nothing more than devising plans to defeat an enemy. When he'd first recruited Frederick as a spy, they would work hours into the night as they examined the strengths and weaknesses of the various solutions they devised.

Lord Cary was a clever man. He understood the motivation that drove a man's choices better than anyone else Frederick had ever met. He could use that uncanny ability to accurately predict how someone would behave given a specific set of external pressures. He always knew exactly which puppet string he needed to pull to evoke the reaction he desired. He was appallingly good at it, and some of the people he manipulated found themselves doing things they'd never dreamed of.

Frederick wasn't as comfortable using such blatant manipulation, nor was he particularly skilled at it. He much preferred devising an overall strategy and then finding key people who best suited his overarching goals. Frederick liked to think his methods were much more subtle and natural than Lord Cary's. Kinder as well.

Lord Cary's manipulations occasionally had the consequence of leaving a man's life in shambles. Sadly, even though Lord Cary could evoke the reaction he wanted, he couldn't foresee the effect of his actions on the poor wretch he'd manipulated.

Lord Cary might predict the precise moment when he could trade some small incentive for a secret or betrayal and use that knowledge to his advantage to gather information, but he couldn't accurately measure the cost of that betrayal on a man's conscience. He sometimes pushed too hard. Too far. Men broke under his pressure. Not frequently, but often enough.

For years, Lord Cary had been oblivious to the havoc he'd caused. After using a man to achieve a specific goal, he forgot about him. At first, Frederick believed Lord Cary to be callous as he casually tore apart a man's life as easily as rending wet tissue paper.

He'd been wrong.

Lord Cary hadn't been callous. He'd been myopic. To him, men were tools, picked up and used as needed, but then cast aside with little thought.

Frederick had come to this realization one day while listening to Lord Cary bemoan the loss of a storeroom guard in the Great Western Railway. Two years earlier he'd bribed the man, convincing him to leave his post for a few minutes. Now, he wanted to get into the same storeroom again, but the new guards weren't so easily manipulated.

"Did they sack him?" Lord Cary asked in a disinterested tone. "That seems a bit harsh. He only left the room unguarded for a few minutes."

Frederick recalled staring at him in stunned disbelief. "Did you think the fact he let one of your spies slip into the room would go unpunished? His employers dismissed him the very same day. Within a month, he was reduced to picking pockets. A month after that, he was in prison."

"That's blasted inconvenient." Lord Cary pinched his lower lip between his thumb and forefinger as he concentrated. "Now the railroad has two guards on duty. I might be able to sway the younger one, but the older man is one of those dedicated sorts. A former army sergeant. Rigid as they come."

Frederick narrowed his eyes. "Wait. Is that all you have to say? You're irritated because you've been inconvenienced after you ruined a man's life?"

Lord Cary stared at him blankly. "I'm afraid I don't know what you're talking about."

Frederick let out a sigh. "I'm referring to the man you bribed. The one who was dismissed."

Confusion fled his face. "Ah. Him." He shook his head. "The man never should have been a guard. He wasn't suited for it. Much too easily bored. He rather enjoyed the excitement of helping one of Her Majesty's spies."

Something cold tightened around Frederick's neck. "I thought you said you bribed him."

"No, no. I was mistaken. I recall the young man quite clearly now. Idealistic. Easily swayed."

"You ruined his life."

"Don't be foolish." Lord Cary's face reddened, but then his voice took on a defensive tone. "He ruined his own life. A man should know his own limitations, don't you think? He wasn't suited for the position of night guard. He should have known that about himself. Life is made of choices. What position to take. Who to marry. Who to help. Whether to turn right or left at a crossroads. Some decisions are minor, and some have enormous consequences. That former night watchman made too many poor ones. I certainly didn't force him to become a pickpocket. If fact, it appears he made yet another poor career choice, given that he ended up in jail so quickly."

"But you manipulated him into losing his job. If not for your interference, he'd probably still be working there."

"Ah. Now I comprehend your meaning." Lord Cary rubbed at

his chin for a moment. "You might be right about that. I found him to be a likable enough fellow, if a bit gullible." He swayed his head from side to side, as if weighing a conclusion. "You're right. Although I doubt he would have remained in his position as a guard for long, I'm fairly certain he never would have turned to a life of crime if he hadn't been sacked." He let out a sigh. "I suppose that when he was dismissed, his employer refused to give him any sort of letter of recommendation."

"You're correct in your supposition. You manipulated him into a desperate position. I thought you already knew all this."

Lord Cary jutted out his lower lip as he shook his head. "No. I don't keep track of all the men I've ever used, but now you're making me wonder if others might have suffered due to my interference in their lives."

"Only now?" Frederick asked, blurting out the question before he could stop himself.

Lord Cary looked startled. "What was that?"

Frederick peered at him more closely. "What will you do now?"

Lord Cary scowled. "I think I'll investigate this further. Although I doubt there's anything I can do to help now that the man is in prison. But there's his family to think about." He shook his head. "Blast it. Now I'm feeling guilty about the way I used him."

Lord Cary's methods had radically changed since that day. He'd become more cautious when manipulating people. In fact, he'd become rather protective of those around him. Frederick believed he now viewed them as extensions of his spy network rather than as disposable items.

Frederick sighed deeply. He hoped Lord Cary would be able to help him with this particular mess. He could use a guiding hand right now.

The way he'd treated Josephine these past few days weighed heavily upon his mind. He knew he should break things off with her, but the simple fact that he couldn't erase her from his thoughts made him doubt the wisdom of his choice. He'd found that after he made a good decision, he could set a problem aside and stop worrying about it. Therefore, cutting her out of his life had been a poor one.

He needed a better solution. One he could live with.

He had two thorny problems to address, but only one had the fate of the nation depending upon it. That one needed to take precedence. Once it was under control, he could address the one closer to his heart.

He knew exactly where to find Lord Cary tonight. The man thrived on gossip. It was like fuel for his espionage network. They rarely met at the Foreign Office. Lord Cary preferred attending social events where he could simultaneously conduct business and collect new tidbits of information. When meeting with someone in his spy network at one of these public venues, he relied upon a code he'd devised. This worked well for providing simple updates, but the in-depth conversation Frederick required tonight would oblige him to schedule a late-night meeting. Probably at Lord Cary's club.

Frederick hurried on his way, and a short time later he strolled into Lord and Lady Aldridge's home for their musical soiree.

The high-ceilinged room with its cream-colored walls hummed with the conversation of elegantly dressed members of the upper class. The women's bell-shaped gowns swayed gracefully as they swept across the room on the arms of men dressed in nearly identical black evening clothes.

Not for the first time, Frederick wondered at Lord Cary's choice of venue. The Aldridges weren't involved in the spymaster's network, but he regularly used their home as a meeting place when they held one of their many social gatherings. In fact, none of the people who hosted events where Frederick met with him were ever directly involved in espionage.

From across the room, he spotted the lovely young soprano

who would entertain them tonight. She and Lady Wilmot, an avid music lover, were engrossed in conversation. If Frederick's brother Robert had been here, he would want to hurry across the room to join them, but not so for Frederick. Tonight's soiree with its musical entertainment was simply a means to an end. He needed to meet Lord Cary, and the Aldridges' event provided a venue.

A moment later, Lady Wilmot and the soprano both turned to face someone, and Frederick realized they were looking directly at Lord Cary.

Well, this was an interesting development. Perhaps Lady Wilmot's presence explained why Lord Cary had chosen this particular event for a rendezvous. He'd seen them together often recently. Could she be one of his spies as well? He hoped not. He liked her too much to wish that sort of life on such an open and honest person. The secrets she'd be forced to keep would eat away at her, much in the same way they did him. He'd become accustomed to that sort of burden at an early age.

Lord Cary caught his gaze and tilted his head, indicating a spot nearby where they should meet. Then he spoke to Lady Wilmot and the young soprano, obviously saying his goodbyes. He casually turned away from them and glided over to intercept Frederick.

"Good to see you, Woolsy." Lord Cary accompanied the greeting with a jovial pat on the back. According to Lord Cary's code, "good to see you" meant it was safe for them to speak.

"I'm running late tonight," he said, letting the man know his assignment hadn't gone well last night.

"Late? You? There's a first for everything." Lord Cary narrowed his eyes. "It's probably your timepiece. I can give you name of an excellent man who can repair it quickly." That was Cary's offer of help.

Frederick nodded. "Is he fast? What's his address?" Those questions let Lord Cary know he wanted to meet right away.

Lord Cary frowned. "I believe it's 1122 Cross Street. I'll check when I get home and send you a letter confirming it."

Of course, "1122" meant they'd meet at Lord Cary's club at around eleven o'clock tonight. Twenty-two meant he might be late.

"It's kind of you to trouble yourself," Frederick replied, agreeing to the appointed time.

From across the room, Frederick caught the flash of that unusual shade of celadon blue. Josephine? Was she here, or was it simply that he couldn't get her out of his mind?

"Admiral, wonderful to see you," Lord Cary said heartily as a man approached them. Frederick took the opportunity to slip away and move closer to the bright spot of color he'd noticed.

The crowd shifted, hiding the woman from view, but it had to be Josephine. The very room seemed to vibrate with her presence.

As though in a choreographed dance, the crowd shifted again. Frederick spotted her not ten feet away. She tilted her head as she smiled up at another man, her blond hair lustrous in the lamplight and her sapphire necklace throwing off reflected glints of light. Then her face softened.

Frederick tensed. She stood next to Lord Temple. Why was she smiling up at him that way? Frederick narrowed his eyes. She'd been talking with the lordling at the embassy last night as well.

Frederick's gaze raked over the slim, brown-haired man. A nice enough fellow, if you liked that type. But he wasn't suited to Josephine. She'd trample him into the ground. She was much too high-spirited and intelligent to be a good match for a man as pleasant and uncomplicated as Lord Temple.

An instant later, Frederick stiffened as Lord Temple casually placed his hand on Josephine's lower back and leaned closer to her cheek. It rankled. The man appeared to be murmuring something in her ear. It took all Frederick's self-control not to storm over there and drag her away.

He forced himself to wait to see how she'd react. She quickly had Lord Temple back under control. It was quite clever of her. She tossed back her head to laugh, shifting away from him so his hand slipped from her waist. Poor Temple seemed transfixed by the arch of her throat.

She glanced over her shoulder and caught Frederick staring at them. A slow, knowing smile spread over her lips before she turned back to face Lord Temple.

A moment later, Lord Temple left her, heading directly toward the refreshment table.

With her chin tilted down, Josephine glanced at Frederick from beneath hooded eyes, beckoning him with her gaze.

Such a tease.

He didn't bother to dawdle as he joined her. She might believe she'd called him over, but he only went because he'd decided to do so. He was perfectly capable of staying away if he so desired.

As he swept up next to her, he didn't pause, but simply took her hand and tucked it into the crook of his arm.

He half-expected her to pull away. He was relieved when she didn't. Instead, she allowed herself to be escorted through the doorway and down the hall to a nearby chamber.

In the dark room, the only light came from the open windows leading to the well-lighted patio. Fortunately, no other guests were outside at the moment. Even if they had been, it was unlikely they'd be able to see into the darkened morning room.

He glanced down at Josephine in the dim light. She was being so biddable. So out of character.

As she stared at him expectantly, he suddenly realized how out of character he was behaving as well. He hadn't even spoken a word to her.

Why had he brought her to this room? He wasn't even certain what had driven him to do so, but when he'd found her, he'd known he needed to be alone with her.

He moved closer. She shifted her weight, flattening her skirts against the heavy desk at her back. She stopped, trapped between him and the leather-topped desk.

Frederick reached out his left hand and touched her waist in exactly the same spot where Lord Temple had touched her. He slowly glided his hand along the warmth of her ribcage.

Her breath caught and she let out a small gasp of surprise at his touch. But she didn't pull away as she had with Lord Temple. Instead, she stared up at him, her mouth slightly open, her lower lip full and soft and... trembling?

The sight of that quavering movement pierced him as nothing else could. He leaned down, unable to resist the temptation of her lips. As their mouths touched, he nearly moaned with the pleasure of it. The warmth of her lips wrapped around him like a dream. His hand tightened at her waist, then he pulled her closer, crushing her body against his. Wanting, nay, craving what she'd freely given him only a week ago.

How had he stayed away from her for so long? How had he convinced himself he could live anything resembling a life without her?

Her hand slid up his chest. She pulled at the lapel of his jacket, then slipped her hand beneath it, flattening it to the spot where his heart thundered. The heat of her palm seared into his skin. Her hand clenched, grabbing hold of his shirt. But only for a moment—an instant later, she flattened it against his chest again.

And pushed.

Frederick stumbled back. Dazed.

She turned her back to him. The pale arch of her neck glowed reproachfully in the soft light. Vulnerable.

As she glanced over her shoulder at him, he saw the pain in her eyes. The confusion. "Frederick, what are you doing? What do you want from me? Is this all I am to you? A plaything?" Her fists clenched in the satin skirt of her gown, crushing the delicate fabric. "Am I nothing more to you than a toy you pull out on a whim and then toss aside again when you're bored?"

Her words struck him like a fistful of snow. The pain in her voice pierced his heart with shards of ice. He shook his head. "Is that what you believe? That I hold you in such low esteem?"

Her eyes seemed to darken with anger as she faced him, planting her hands on her hips. "What else am I to think? You court me for nearly a year until I can no longer resist you, and once you've had me, you avoid me. Or should I say, you avoid me until you see me with another man."

"Lord Temple? You think I'm jealous of that specimen? That's ridiculous. He's so malleable you already have him dancing to your tune." He regretted the words as soon as he'd spoken them.

A sharp smile cut across her face. "I saw you arrive," she said. "You didn't notice me at first, but once you did, the look you gave Lord Temple was a telling one. Do you dislike him so very much?"

She'd been able to read that in him? Frederick pressed his lips together. Had he lost control over his emotions where she was concerned, or was she particularly skilled at interpreting his facial expressions? "Are you suggesting that I'm so awkward and inelegant that I broadcast my every emotion for the world to see?"

Her stern expression softened as she gathered her hands at her waist. "Not to worry, master spy. It's only because I've come to know you so well." Her face tightened again. "Which means I know you well enough to recognize when you're toying with me."

He flinched from her words. "I'd never treat you so shabbily. I know I've lost your trust, but I hope you'll believe me when I say I hold you in the highest esteem."

She narrowed her eyes, examining his face, and then gave a terse nod. "You believe what you're saying. That doesn't mean you're telling me the entire truth. I don't believe you know your own mind where I'm concerned."

Frederick let out a huff of frustration. "You believe me but you don't believe me? Is that what you're saying? Isn't that a bit contradictory?" She turned her face to one side, but her hurt and confusion slammed into him. He'd done this to her. He reached out to stroke her neck with the back of his fingertips. "What man truly knows his own heart, especially where a woman is concerned?"

She shivered and reflexively bent her cheek toward his hand. Then she pulled away. "Many. But it takes being truthful to yourself. I don't think you're particularly adept at that."

A flush swept over his face. She wanted truth. How could he convince her he wanted the same thing between them? "I—my brother and I called on the Russian ambassador today," he blurted out. "I thought you might want to be kept apprised of our progress."

She stilled. "Does the ambassador suspect Robert stole the book?"

Frederick dragged his fingers through his hair. "That was our first assumption when his men tried to kidnap Robert off the street last night."

"What?" Her eyes widened. "Did they harm him?"

Frederick shook his head. "We thought it best to confront Ambassador Revnik immediately so we could address his suspicions, but it turned out he didn't believe we'd stolen it." He gave her a faint smile. "He was after the real thief. A woman in a silver gown. He knew exactly who she was and hoped we could provide information about her."

Josephine rubbed at her forehead. "Does that mean she's a spy?"

Frederick swung his head from side to side. "I don't think so. The ambassador said something strange. Apparently the woman is 'too important' for him to question directly. He preferred trying to kidnap an earl. Can you make any sense of that? Because I can't."

"More important than an earl? That's interesting. Who is she?"

"I still don't know. Based on Robert's description, she's British, cultured, and is skilled at deception. I originally assumed she must be a spy, but now I'm beginning to reconsider. She isn't one of ours, and she clearly doesn't work for the Russians. Perhaps she's working for the French." He closed his eyes and shook his head in frustration. "If only I could locate her. It's frustrating she was able to disappear like mist."

He let out a sigh as he stepped back from her. "We should rejoin the other guests before your absence is noted."

She reached up and smoothed his hair in place. "That's better. You were looking a bit tousled."

"I trust you won't reveal any of this."

She scowled at him. "Of course not. Honestly, Frederick. Do you think I'm featherbrained?"

"It's not—of course—"

She said nothing, but swept past him and yanked open the door. He hurried to catch up. At the door leading back to the gathering, he offered her his arm.

She stared at it for a moment, and he could sense her indecision. She couldn't decide if she wanted to reenter the salon alone, or with him.

"It will look less suspicious if nothing seems amiss between us."

She frowned as she grudgingly placed her hand on his arm. "I'm not a ninny," she muttered.

"I'm sorry," he said.

She ignored him.

As they reentered the room, Frederick glanced around, but no one seemed to take note of their entrance. Not even Lord Temple, who was speaking with another gentleman, Mr. Easterly. As Frederick watched, Lord Temple gave Mr. Easterly a polite nod and turned toward the refreshment table.

Josephine watched him for a moment as well, and then offered Frederick a tight smile. She cleared her throat. When she spoke, her voice took on a formal quality, as though she assumed people were eavesdropping. "I hadn't expected you to be here tonight. Is your hand improved?"

"The poultice helped," he replied in a similar formal tone, "but I'm nearly out of the supplies."

"Mrs. Drummer will prepare more for you tomorrow. I'd be happy to bring them to you."

Frederick tensed.

Josephine narrowed her eyes the tiniest bit. "Unless you don't want them."

"Of course I want them." He glanced pointedly at Lord Temple across the room. The man picked up two glasses of punch from the refreshment table. "But perhaps you shouldn't bring them yourself. Lord Temple might not approve."

She narrowed her eyes as she lifted her chin. He could see the tug of irritation and disapproval at the corner of her mouth. "You *are* jealous, aren't you? And this is your way of trying to discern my feelings for him. Don't bother. It's none of your concern. I don't report to you, *Mr. Woolsy*."

A hot flash of something seared through him. Jealousy? Of course not. It was irritation, plain and simple. Irritation with Josephine for turning what should have been a pleasant evening into something else. Something much more complicated.

Josephine glanced at Lord Temple as he approached them and then flicked her gaze over Frederick. "Is it possible you've come to realize you care for me after all? It's either that, or you merely wish to control me. I can't quite decide which it is." She gazed into his eyes, as if trying to read the answer in them. After a moment, she gave up, shaking her head. "It appears you aren't certain of the answer to that question either."

Something intense and visceral tightened in his chest. He wanted to snap back a reply. He wanted to pull her into his arms again, just as he'd done a few moments ago. He wanted to banish that half-smile from her mouth by scorching it away with his lips and leaving her flushed and in no doubt that she wanted him and only him.

But what he wanted rarely matched what he actually did.

So he smiled benignly, leashing the jealousy—yes, jealousy—that smoldered in his chest.

"Your refreshment, Lady Harrington." Lord Temple passed her a glass filled with a frothy pink liquid.

Frederick nodded to them both. "Please pass along my thanks to Mrs. Drummer, and let her know I'm looking forward to her delivery tomorrow."

And he turned away.

6

Lord Temple glanced across the room. "He's still watching you."

Josephine gave him a brittle smile. "I told you, Tristan. He's jealous of you." She sipped from her punch glass.

Tristan leaned over and murmured into her ear, "If only he knew."

She batted her eyes. "That you have no interest in pursuing me?"

Tristan shrugged, his muscles rolling beneath his evening coat so that it tightened across his shoulders. "That I feel as though I'm using you."

"We're using each other, so it negates the effect. Thank you for agreeing to be my escort so often."

She glanced at Frederick, and he immediately looked away. He appeared quite irritated with her. Good. He deserved it after treating her so shabbily. One corner of her mouth drew up in an unladylike smirk before she smoothed it away. She finished off her punch and set the empty glass on a passing footman's tray.

A devilish gleam lit Tristan's eye. "You certainly put poor Frederick in a bother," he commented. "Would you like to let him cool off for a while, or would you prefer to raise him to a simmer?"

She smiled and lifted one eyebrow. "Simmering sounds intriguing. What did you have in mind?"

"This." He stared directly at Frederick and scowled darkly. He grabbed Josephine by the elbow and hurried her from the room.

Josephine nearly stumbled in her haste to keep up with him, but his firm grip kept her upright. She glanced around, but fortunately, the other guests didn't appear to take note of their dash for the door. Instead, they were turning to focus on their host.

"If you will please take your seats, Miss Bonneville will begin her performance shortly," Lord Aldridge said.

"What are you doing?" Josephine asked Tristan through tight lips.

"Adding a bit of heat. Frederick is watching us, isn't he?"

She glanced back and caught Frederick's scowl. "He looks angry."

"That means my plan is working," He rushed her back into the corridor she'd just been in with Frederick. "Your Lothario should be along momentarily."

She shook her head. "I don't understand."

"Play along," he said softly. He flashed her a dashing smile, but an instant later he scowled. "You can't send me off for a refreshment and then disappear with another man."

She stared at him blankly. "What on earth...?"

He frowned at her. "I said, play along," he whispered.

Comprehension washed over her. She squared her shoulders, scowled at him, and yanked her elbow from his grasp. "Need I remind you, you are not my husband, Lord Temple. Only my father and my husband ever had the right to tell me what I can and cannot do, and they're both gone now. It is not your place to assume that role."

Frederick stepped through the doorway, his jaw tight.

Tristan scowled at him as he took a step closer to Josephine, edging between her and Frederick. "Am I supposed to ignore the fact you left in his carriage at the Koliada Ball?"

She blushed at that. "He was injured."

"Yet he's here tonight. Apparently your ministrations wrought a miraculous recovery."

She felt her blush deepening. She didn't like this pretense. It felt wrong. Manipulative.

"Stop talking about me as though I'm not here." Frederick said. "And stop trying to intimidate Lady Harrington. You're lucky you haven't drawn a crowd." He glanced over his shoulder, but from what Josephine could see through the doorway, all the other guests were focused on Lord Aldridge at the other end of the room.

"*Now* you're concerned about drawing unwanted notice?" The corner of Tristan's eye twitched convincingly. "Perhaps you should have thought of that before you drove away from the ball with her in your carriage, or before you trotted her out the door a few minutes ago." Tristan looked furious. If she hadn't been in on the ruse, she would have been utterly fooled.

Josephine shot a scorching glare that took in the pair of them. "I've had enough of this ridiculous scene." She sidestepped Tristan and began moving toward the door. "I came here tonight to listen to Miss Bonneville perform, not hear the pair of you yowl at each other like angry tomcats."

"I only wanted to protect you," Frederick said as he reached out to take her by the arm.

She easily evaded his grasp. "I can protect myself. Please leave me alone. Both of you."

She swept through the doorway and back into the now quiet room. She'd ended that scene none too soon. One moment longer and they would have become tonight's entertainment and upstaged Miss Bonneville.

In the row of chairs lined up for the performance, she spotted a solitary vacant seat in the front row and claimed it. Neither man would be able to follow her here.

Nearly an hour later, Josephine applauded vigorously following Miss Bonneville's last encore. The soprano's voice was extraordinary, and her vocal range was astonishing.

Josephine was thankful she'd had the time to regain her composure. She never should have agreed to Tristan's ruse. It had been foolish and childish, and it had been her own fault. After all, Tristan had asked if she wanted to make Frederick simmer.

She'd certainly achieved that particular goal.

As people rose to their feet, she glanced around the room, but she couldn't find Frederick. Had he left?

She quickly spotted Tristan. When she caught his eye, he slipped through the crowd toward her.

"Did he leave?" she asked.

"I think so, but I'm not certain."

They both scanned the room, but Frederick was nowhere to be found.

Tristan stiffened, and then his countenance became carefully composed. "Would you like some punch?" His eyes remained locked on something as he spoke. "You must be parched."

Josephine followed his gaze, noting the elegantly clad man standing alone near the punch bowl. Not something. Some*one*. Mr. Easterly, to be specific. "As a matter of fact, I would," she said, not really expecting the glass of punch to ever materialize. She was certain Tristan would become much too distracted. He'd helped her with Frederick. Now it was her turn to help him with his relationship with Mr. Easterly.

He smiled, his gaze intent on the other man as he headed toward him. Mr. Easterly noticed his approach and something brightened in his gaze. She doubted she'd be drinking punch within the next thirty minutes.

She spotted Lady Wilmot across the room and moved to join her.

"Good evening, Lady Harrington," the older woman said. "Didn't you simply adore the performance? Miss Bonneville is truly gifted."

"Indeed," Josephine replied. "I heard her last month at the Palmertons' soiree. I understand she'll have the title role in *Lucia di Lammermoor* next month."

"Oh, my. Yes. I'm so looking forward to it. My late husband used to dearly love Lucia's mad scene."

"Such a tragic story of treachery and ill-fated love," Josephine commented. "Poor Lucia, to be lied to and manipulated by the people she trusted." The irony of that statement wasn't lost on her. She pressed her lips in a thin line.

"The opera stands as a lesson for humanity for those willing to learn," Lady Wilmot said, nodding sagely. "No good can come from trying to manipulate someone for selfish reasons." Then a brilliant smile blazed across the older woman's face. "But still, that mad scene is something to behold."

Josephine chuckled at Lady Wilmot's enthusiasm. "That it is."

Lady Wilmot caught her daughter's eye and beckoned her over. "I was just telling Lady Harrington about *Lucia di Lammermoor*. I'm trying to recall if you ever attended a performance of it."

Lady Elizabeth shook her head. "No. I was too young when you and Father went, but I heard him speak of it so often, I feel as though I attended it too. I'll never forget the night you invited the soprano to perform it for your musical soiree. I fully intended to remain hidden in the balcony and listen, but once I heard her voice, I couldn't resist slipping downstairs and watching through the doorway."

"You didn't!" Lady Wilmot looked horrified. "What if someone had seen you?"

Lady Elizabeth blushed. "I managed to avoid everyone. Don't worry, Mother, I was careful."

Josephine watched Elizabeth carefully. She was lying.

Josephine was certain of it. Someone had seen her. But why lie about that one detail when she'd been willing to reveal she'd watched it?

She was getting better at spotting lies. She'd gained a great deal of experience this past year through observing an expert. Frederick was a challenge, but Lady Elizabeth was relatively easy to read.

Lady Wilmot shook her head and frowned in disapproval. "A young woman in your position has to be careful. After all, this is your second—"

"My second season. Or perhaps even my third, if you count the two weeks I was in London before I left to be with my aunt."

"Don't say such a thing. It's your second." Lady Wilmot glanced anxiously at Josephine, as though looking for her support.

"I agree with your mother. That first year didn't count. Your time here was so brief. You'd barely arrived before you had to leave."

Something across the room caught Lady Wilmot's attention. She pursed her lips. "If you'll excuse me," she said.

"Of course." Josephine watched her as she joined an older gentleman. Lord Cary, if she wasn't mistaken.

"My mother is overly concerned about appearances," Lady Elizabeth commented.

"I wonder if that's a requirement for motherhood," Josephine said. "Mine was the same way. Being a widow is quite liberating." She blushed. "I'm afraid I sounded coldhearted. I didn't mean it that way. Of course I wish Lord Harrington were still with us, but he isn't. I'm done mourning and I've moved on with my life. Now I enjoy much more freedom than I did when I was having my season. I wouldn't give it up for just anyone."

Elizabeth glanced over at where Tristan was in conversation with young Mr. Easterly. "Lord Temple and Mr. Easterly have an extremely close friendship. Does that trouble you?"

Josephine glanced at her sharply. Surely someone as young as

Lady Elizabeth couldn't guess at the sort of relationship the two men shared. "Certainly not. Mr. Easterly is quite pleasant."

Elizabeth focused on Josephine, appraising her. "Are you aware that Lord Temple has no interest in marrying or creating any heirs? He's already designated his nephew as next in line for his title."

Josephine couldn't suppress her smile. Obviously Elizabeth was aware of Tristan's lack of interest in women. "You're much more well-informed than I would have guessed from someone with such an overprotective mother."

Elizabeth smirked. "What do you think drove her to become so overprotective? I've always been extremely curious about the people I meet." She glanced at Tristan again. "Are you using him to keep other men at bay?"

"It's a mutually agreed upon arrangement."

"And where does that leave Mr. Woolsy?"

Josephine pressed her lips together. "That's the question, isn't it? Or the better one might be, does Mr. Woolsy know where he wants to be?"

❦ 7 ❧

After his confrontation with Josephine and Lord Temple, Frederick realized he wasn't behaving rationally. Not only had he dragged her away to a secluded room to seduce her, but he'd also given in to a fit of jealous rage and confronted Lord Temple in the hallway. Both those actions were completely out of character. He planned. He considered. He did not rush into any situation without first weighing his options and considering the consequences.

The thought of losing his composure at a social event was abhorrent, but he simply couldn't trust himself. Not tonight. Not around Josephine. If he stayed, he might do something reckless again.

He decided to walk from Lord Aldridge's home to the Ambridge Club. The brisk activity helped soothe his anger, and by the time he trotted up the building's front steps and passed his coat and hat to one of the footmen, he'd regained his composure. All it had taken was banishing Josephine from his thoughts.

It was only half-past ten when he settled into one of a pair of leather chairs in a secluded corner of the club. The supple leather carried the faint scents of beeswax and almond oil.

On the far side of the room, an enormous glowing fireplace large enough for a man to stand in provided plenty of heat. Near it, Lord Larchmont held court, surrounded by his sycophants. He was a man who bore watching. He portrayed himself as a patriot, but Frederick knew him too well. If Lord Larchmont believed he wouldn't be caught, he'd be more than willing to betray his country—for the right price. With that man, everything had a price. Even his own daughters. He'd actually married off his eldest to a violent man in exchange for political favors. Despicable.

Tonight, Frederick watched the group closely, but he detected nothing unusual taking place. That didn't allay his suspicions. He observed, noting the shifting friendships and alliances among the man's followers. Each person in Lord Larchmont's circle had influence, which was why he'd chosen each one to add to his collection. Something of interest always took place when these men gathered together. All he had to do was watch.

Over the years, Frederick had learned the art of surveillance. It had become second nature to him. If something unusual occurred, no matter how small or subtle, he'd notice.

Perhaps his habit explained why he'd been achingly aware of Lord Temple's attraction to Josephine. Every glance, every gesture, every word the man uttered had been chosen to impress her.

But Josephine only toyed with him. She pulled him in with a word or a glance, but kept him at a distance with a combination of stiffness and propriety. She'd likely driven the poor man mad.

She'd never played those games with Frederick. But then again, when it came to Josephine, he wondered if he might have a strange, unexpected blindness for her alone. She'd always seemed completely genuine. Perhaps that explained why he'd finally given in to temptation a week ago and shared those two blissful nights in her bed.

He'd loved her openness. Her honesty. Most people were filled with guile.

So why had she been filled with deceit tonight? Her every interaction with Lord Temple had been brimming with mixed signals and subterfuge. Had Frederick finally noticed it because he'd been an observer rather than a player in the scene? Had he fallen so deeply under her spell that he hadn't noticed when she'd woven the same threads of trickery around him? He shook his head. That wasn't possible. She might have been able to mislead him on one or two occasions, but he'd known her for over a year. He simply couldn't believe she could deceive him for so long.

He couldn't have misjudged her so thoroughly.

Subtle movements made by two young men standing to the right of the enormous fireplace across the room caught his attention. Their demeanor changed as they became wary of being overheard and moved to one side. One of the young men passed a piece of paper to the other.

Frederick recognized the yellow slip as coming from one of the gambling houses. A gaming debt, so it would seem. Had it been paid off, or was one of the men selling a debt to the other?

Occasionally debts were sold at a discount. The seller would get ready cash, and the purchaser could choose either to attempt to recover the debt, or to use the marker to manipulate the debtor in other, more insidious ways.

Frederick made a mental note to investigate. The exchange might be innocent, but people could do foolish things when blackmailed, and with war in the Crimean Peninsula looming, Frederick wouldn't take any chances. Especially since the one paying the debt was the son of the minister of war.

Lord Cary claimed the chair next to him. "I've been watching them for a few weeks. This isn't the first time he's bought those markers."

Frederick smiled inwardly. Of course Lord Cary knew what was happening. It exemplified the new way he viewed the world after that debacle with the night guard—as though everyone in his purview was his responsibility. From his point of view as the spymaster, these two young men *were* his responsibility—especially the war minister's son. "Would you like me to investigate further?"

"I already have. It isn't anything to worry about. The young viscount is paying off his brother's gambling debts. It's a useless endeavor. The pup already found a new hellhole willing to accept his credit and last night he negated all his brother's progress with one long, unlucky stint at roulette." Lord Cary shook his head. "The boy needs discipline—he needs to be challenged. I told his father that a couple of years in the army would help straighten him out. The last thing that young pup needs is for his older brother to clean up his messes."

Frederick nodded. "Do you plan to continue monitoring the situation?"

Lord Cary stilled for a moment. Another man might have found the ensuing pause negligible, but to Frederick, that brief silence was as obvious as a shout. He focused entirely upon his mentor. Lord Cary was about to say something of utmost importance.

"Since this situation is incidental to my main responsibilities, I'll keep an eye on things. But as for the bulk of my responsibilities, I plan to pass them along to someone else. That's why I wanted to talk with you tonight. I plan to step down as spymaster."

Frederick stared at him in stunned silence. It took a moment for him to find his words. "Now?" He shook his head in confusion. "Given the situation with Russia, your role is vital. You can't leave now. War is all but certain."

"Which is exactly why this is the best time to make this decision. If we go to war, it would be irresponsible of me to leave. Even if we don't, the Eastern Question will remain unresolved."

Frederick's stomach turned over. The church register he'd lost last night might be the key to averting that war. The Eastern Question was another matter entirely. At issue was the power vacuum created by the fall of the Ottoman Empire. What government would step forward in the eastern countries and provide the stability so sorely needed? England? Japan? France? Russia had decided to make its move. If they succeeded, how would that change the balance of power throughout the world?

"I can influence the choice of my successor. I prefer it to be you. Despite your youth, you're perfectly suited for the role. Years ago, you surpassed me in evaluating threats and predicting outcomes. Your achievements are legendary"—he smiled shrewdly —"for those few who are privileged to know about them." He watched Frederick. "There's no one I'd prefer to take my place. Does the opportunity appeal to you?"

Heat rose in Frederick's face. He'd never liked praise. It seemed fleeting and too often insincere. However, Lord Cary never flattered. A compliment from him was as rare as an honest man. He swallowed. "You've managed to astonish me." The corner of his mouth turned up in a wry smile as he let out a huff of self-deprecating laughter. "Your praise is unfounded. My reaction to your news proves it. If I'm your foremost expert in predicting outcomes, why didn't I foresee this?"

Lord Cary's mouth turned up on one side, mirroring Frederick's smile. "Because I happen to be very good at keeping secrets and concealing my plans."

Something in the man's voice made Frederick peer at Lord Cary more closely. What he saw made him realize he hadn't truly examined the spymaster in months. Now he took note of the signs of stress he'd formerly dismissed. With dawning awareness, Frederick realized he'd become complacent where his mentor was concerned—or perhaps he hadn't wanted to acknowledge the truth. The man had aged. The lines of fatigue creasing his face had deepened over the past few months.

He looked at Lord Cary with fresh eyes, registering what he should have seen all along. The signs of sadness and exhaustion he found shouldn't come as such a shock to him. After all, Lord

Cary's wife had died three years ago. Frederick should have paid closer attention. "Are you sure this is what you want?"

"It's time. I can feel it."

Frederick shook his head. "I dreamed of becoming spymaster someday, but I never imagined the opportunity would arise so soon."

"Too soon?"

Frederick paused. A band of tension tightened around his chest. Did he want this? "You know I'd prefer that you stay."

Lord Cary only stared at him. A certain resolute determination seemed to settle over his features as if they were carved in stone.

Frederick let out a sigh. "I can see you've made your decision." The tension in his chest released, allowing him to breathe more deeply. Now that the idea was before him, he wanted it. Wanted it desperately. "If you're determined to leave, I'd relish the opportunity to succeed you."

Lord Cary gave that satisfied smile Frederick had often seen when one of his predictions came true. "I thought so." Then he sobered. "But we seem to have a problem. Many of the men who will choose my successor won't know of your long record of excellence. Your recent achievements will heavily influence their decision."

Frederick thought back over the past few months, but nothing struck him as being an issue—except—

Lord Cary nodded. "You see the problem. It's essential you recover that book. Let's put our heads together and devise a plan."

THEY TALKED WELL INTO THE SMALL HOURS OF THE MORNING as Frederick and Lord Cary devised alternatives for recovering the book. Given the unknown identity of the thief, none of their ideas were particularly solid or satisfying. They examined theories regarding her identity and then devised strategies for flushing her from wherever she might be hiding. Lord Cary agreed there was a good chance she was French, but it was only guesswork at this point.

Finally, Lord Cary rose to his feet. "I need some sleep. Meet me at the Foreign Office at nine o'clock. I need to introduce you to some men. They'll be the ones who will make the final decision regarding my successor."

He reached out to shake Frederick's hand, but then pulled back. "Sorry about your injuries." He shook his head. "Lord Percival showed so much promise when he was young. It's a shame he became such a wastrel. I considered interfering a few years ago when I recognized the self-destructive path he'd chosen. It's too bad I didn't. It's one of my bigger regrets. If I had, you might not have been burned last night."

Frederick let out a chuckle. "An unexpected event can destroy even the best of plans. No one could have predicted the Lord Percival effect."

Lord Cary let out a low rumble of laughter. "Which is why I always make contingency plans." He touched his finger to the side of his nose. "As you well know."

Frederick dipped his head. "A habit I learned from you."

Lord Cary smiled. "Which explains why you've been so successful." He gave a sharp nod. "I'll see you in a few short hours. Don't be late, and don't miss the appointment. I must leave London soon, and I'll be gone for a fortnight."

He strode from the room as Frederick watched him leave. There were different kinds of stress in life. There was that immediate and direct stress of a life-threatening situation. Frederick had come to know it well over the past few years. But there was also the ever-present stress involved in knowing that others depended upon you.

Lord Cary had learned to balance those long-term burdens

during his career. Some were the simple, day-to-day needs of daily life. Concerns for wife, family, health. But more troubling were the demands placed on him by the network of spies who were his responsibility. They often faced life-or-death situations that demanded Lord Cary's intervention.

In contrast, Frederick's primary responsibility was to the success of his own missions. The only life he put at risk was his own. The rush of danger and excitement he felt could be heady, and it often left him unable to relax for hours afterward, but that was the extent of his emotional burden. He wasn't the sort to berate himself for errors—instead, he learned from them and focused his mental energy on planning for every reasonable contingency in his upcoming missions. If a plan went awry, it was usually due to something he couldn't have foreseen.

Something like Lord Percival.

Lord Cary's worries were of a different magnitude. He didn't place *himself* at risk, but others. And with multiple missions taking place simultaneously, he never had a moment when he could truly relax.

With Frederick's penchant for planning—some might even say over-planning—how would he function as spymaster? He'd be obliged to work with men who had significantly different approaches to completing their assignments. That meant he'd have to accept that he couldn't control the outcomes.

He considered the other spies who worked with Lord Cary. He knew none of them particularly well. Lord Cary preferred to keep the members of his network separated so they wouldn't be compromised.

Frederick normally worked alone, taking on the more subtle and challenging assignments. Although the other spies he'd met prepared strategies for achieving their goals, none of them devoted as much time and energy to devising alternatives as he did. And none of them had achieved his consistent level of success either.

Could he adjust his standards? Could he accept that others would approach their missions in a more haphazard manner? His jaw tightened at the mere idea of making such a compromise.

Perhaps he was asking himself the wrong question. What if he raised his expectations? What if he taught his network of spies how to search out and eliminate the failure points in their plans?

Some of his tension eased. This alternative was a good one. The more he turned it over in his mind, the more it appealed to him.

Being spymaster would bring other changes as well. Lord Cary had lived in London and maintained his broad network of spies from the comfort of his own home. He'd even been married. On most nights, the man had been fortunate enough to sleep in his own bed, and that was much more than could be said for Frederick. His assignments had taken him all over England and beyond.

Frederick tipped his head back against the leather chair. He couldn't imagine a more perfect life. A master of spies—a manipulator of destiny. As he pictured himself in the role, a slow, satisfied smile spread across his face.

There was only one addition that could make this fantasy approach perfection.

Having Josephine by his side.

Seizing this opportunity could change his life.

A BEAM OF EARLY-MORNING SUNLIGHT PIERCED THE WINDOW OF the Ambridge Club and woke Frederick. As he stirred, one of the omnipresent footmen approached him. "May I offer you some tea? Breakfast is being served in the dining room."

Frederick rubbed at his face with his left hand, momentarily disoriented by his surroundings. "What time is it?"

"Just past eight o'clock, sir."

Frederick's stomach clenched. He had an appointment at the

Foreign Office this morning. "Blast it. I'll be late. Send for a hackney."

"Certainly, sir. I'll fetch your coat and hat as well."

A short time later, Frederick leaped out of his hackney and ran toward the front door of Woolsy House.

"Wait here," he called to the driver without breaking stride. "I'll be back in a moment." His right hand burned like the devil, but he wouldn't be able to replace the poultice—not if he wanted to meet Lord Cary on time.

He couldn't regret staying at the Ambridge Club since he'd used the time he'd saved by not going home to examine the opportunity Lord Cary had offered him. Nor could he regret the brief hours of sleep he'd stolen there.

He wasn't sure who was more surprised as he burst into the foyer—himself or Robert.

His brother gaped at him. "I don't think I've ever seen you come in at this hour before."

Frederick scowled. He couldn't waste time assuaging his brother's curiosity. Not if he wanted to be on time for his appointment with Lord Cary. "What concern is it of yours?" he asked in a brusque tone, intent on avoiding any further questions. He rushed toward the staircase, bumping his shoulder against Robert's as he brushed past.

"I'll wager this has something to do with Lady Harrington."

Something cold and tight gathered in Frederick's chest. By taking Josephine to his bed last weekend, he'd thoughtlessly exposed her to exactly this sort of assumption, and Robert's careless words raked against his raw emotions. At this moment, he detested himself.

He spun on his brother with fury to find Robert smiling in an obnoxious and knowing way. He clenched his fists and then winced at the pain. "Have a care, brother. You should know better than to sully a lady's name that way. I'm in a hurry right now, or I'd teach you some manners." He took a deep breath, reining in his anger. It was only then that he realized Robert was preparing to leave the house as well. His brows drew together as his curiosity grabbed hold of him. "Where are you going at such an early hour?"

Robert opened his mouth to answer, but Frederick held his palm out, interrupting what might be a long-winded reply.

"It doesn't matter." Frederick dropped his hand, slashing the air between them. "I don't have time to listen to you. I have a meeting at the Foreign Office, and I'll be pressed to arrive on time."

Robert lifted his cane toward Frederick in a sweeping gesture. "Your evening clothes are likely to raise a few eyebrows."

Frederick scowled. Just as he'd feared, Robert was delaying him. "That's why I'm here. To change." He turned on his heel and hurried up the staircase. "I'm too busy to spar with you."

As Frederick burst into his bedroom, his valet, Herbert, covered a bowl with a cloth and turned to face him. "Good morning, sir."

"I'm in a rush. I'm late for a meeting and I need to change."

"Yes, sir." Herbert quickly pulled clothing from the wardrobe while Frederick removed his gloves, coat, and shirt. Herbert had placed a fresh pitcher of water next to a basin, and Frederick poured water into the basin. He splashed the tepid water over his chest and clumsily rubbed the bar of soap with one hand, generating a bit of lather. It took him less than a minute to wash, and he immediately felt better.

He turned to face Herbert, and the man tossed him a clean towel. Frederick snatched it from the air and rubbed himself dry. It only took a moment to don a fresh shirt and jacket.

Herbert turned to face him, holding the bowl he'd been covering when Frederick had first entered the room. With a flourish, he whisked away the white cloth. Inside, Frederick spotted the freshly mashed leaves for his poultice.

Relief cascaded down his spine. "You're priceless. The best valet ever."

Herbert smiled. "I do my best, sir. I saw you arrive in a hackney. You appeared to be in a rush, so I took the liberty of preparing the poultice." He gestured toward the bowl of mashed greenery. "This is the last of the leaves."

Three minutes later, Frederick's entire outlook was transformed. A fresh shirt, a bit of Mrs. Drummer's herbal remedy, and a positive attitude would take him far. With a bit of luck, they would take him all the way to the role of spymaster.

"Wish me luck. I could use a bit extra today."

"Of course, sir. Good luck, sir."

Frederick tore down the staircase and registered his brother's presence as he rushed out the door.

For a brief moment, he wondered why Robert would still be lingering near the entrance, but then he pushed the question from his mind. He needed to stay focused. Lord Cary would expect nothing less.

8

Josephine woke early but lingered in bed. Lately, she always woke to thoughts of Frederick. Did she dream about him every night? Her hand slid across her breast, grazing her erect nipple and sending a shiver of awareness to her core. He did this to her in her dreams, and she always awoke feeling aroused and restless. Needing him next to her. Craving his touch.

At the sound of her doorknob turning, her eyes flew open and she pulled her covers up higher.

Taylor, her maid, backed into the room holding a tray laden with breakfast foods. She carefully balanced it on her hip as she scurried inside and kicked the door closed behind her.

"I brought your breakfast, my lady. That cat of yours followed me all the way upstairs." The glance she shot back at the now-rattling door was both indulgent and mildly irritated. The feline seemed determined to get into the room. "She loves your smoked salmon. She's given me the devil of a time trying to keep her away from it this morning."

Josephine scooted up in bed and rearranged her pillows so she could sit comfortably. "Poor Domino. It's her weakness. I'll wager that if I put my mind to it, I could teach her to jump through a hoop as long as I used smoked salmon as a reward."

Taylor shook her head. "Not that one. I've never seen a more stubborn, independent cat." She lowered the tray's short legs and set it so it balanced above Josephine's lap.

"That may be true, but I don't think she'd stand on principle with her favorite treat hanging in the balance." Josephine picked up the small metal egg-shaped tea strainer and slipped it into her pot of hot water to let it steep.

"Shall I lay out your clothes for the day?"

Josephine placed a slice of the smoked salmon on a triangle of toast. "I want the gown with the white trim at the neckline," she said, and bit into the wedge with a satisfying crunch.

Taylor pulled a celadon-blue gown with snowy-white trim from the wardrobe and examined it as Josephine took a bite of her egg.

Josephine stared at the gown. Once she'd set aside her widow's weeds a year ago, she'd chosen a new wardrobe, and on a whim, she'd had every gown made in celadon blue. A reminder of happier times. Of dreams for the future.

"It needs pressing," Taylor said. "I'll bring it back shortly, m'lady."

Josephine nodded, her mouth full. She waved Taylor away as she swallowed her second triangle of smoked salmon and toast.

As Taylor opened the door, a white streak tore through it.

"Oh, no. Domino!"

"Don't worry about it. I've nearly finished eating my salmon."

Domino jumped onto the bed, stalking the fishy scent. She paused only briefly to glance at Josephine before continuing on.

"Who's my good girl?" Josephine crooned. She put a sliver of smoked salmon on her fingertip and held it out for the cat. Domino delicately accepted it and then dropped to the floor to eat it.

"You spoil that cat."

"Fiddlesticks. She isn't spoiled. She always asks for permission before she takes anything. Didn't you see the way she looked at me first?"

Taylor snorted. "She just wanted to make sure you wouldn't swat her away."

Domino jumped back onto the bed, ready for more fish. As Taylor left the room, she shook her head and clucked her tongue.

Josephine wondered if she'd make a terrible mother. Too lenient. But her own parents had been kind and supportive, and she'd turned out well.

Of course, to be properly done, motherhood required a husband. Unfortunately, she was decidedly lacking in one.

The late Lord Harrington had died two years before in a hunting accident. She suspected alcohol had played a part in the mishap. John's compatriots from the outing had volunteered little information, but she could spot a fabricated story easily enough. Their combination of bare facts along with identical bits of description betrayed their complicity. They'd clearly rehearsed their story.

Her marriage to John had been no love match. She'd known him too short a time to develop strong feelings. Mother had said they'd come with time. Perhaps they would have. She'd tried to care for him, really she had, but she'd only managed to cultivate a mild affection for him.

It shamed her that she'd recovered so easily from losing him. She'd wanted more from their marriage. She'd always dreamed of an epic love. What girl didn't? But all they'd ultimately shared had been something tepid and unsatisfying.

She set aside her breakfast tray and climbed out of bed. Domino jumped onto the side table to examine the remains of the meal, sniffing in disappointment when she didn't find any more smoked salmon.

As if drawn forward by a string, Josephine crossed the room toward her little curio cabinet. It contained a number of oddments she'd collected over the years. She'd intended to add many more interesting items during her travels. She'd planned to visit Egypt, Greece, Istanbul, Rome... so many, many places. She loved learning about ancient cultures. Studying the remains of civilizations. Visiting ancient cities—their monuments and tombs —had been her dream since childhood, but those dreams had never materialized. Marriage had put an end to them.

She stared now at the robin's nest at the center of the glass-and-metal cabinet. Her first curiosity, brought home from her trip across the Atlantic to New England when she'd been a girl. Her parents had taken her there to see some of the world and to visit her uncle and cousins.

She'd fallen in love with the bedroom she'd used during her visit. A red-chested bird built a nest in the tree just outside her window. This nest.

The bird's quick, sharp movements and the flash of its red breast caught Josephine's attention from the outset. She watched it work all day, not wanting to leave her bedroom. It created a frame of dried grass. Then it added a layer of mud to the interior that worked as a sort of glue to hold the bits together. It finished by lining the nest with more bits of dried grass.

A few days later, the bird laid the most beautiful celadon-blue eggs—a unique shade that was soft yet intense. She'd never seen anything like them before. After the robins hatched, she scrabbled through the rough grass beneath the nest to collect the broken fragments of blue shells—her most precious treasure from that trip.

The fledglings hadn't stayed long. A short two weeks after they hatched, they disappeared. She'd been heartbroken. When Uncle Martin found her in tears, he'd climbed out the window and retrieved the nest for her.

When her quiet tears turned into wails of grief, he scrambled back inside through the window, clutching his prize. With patience and effort, he managed learn why.

"I wanted to watch a new family of robins hatch in the nest." Josephine could barely make herself understood through her hiccupping sobs. "Now they won't ever come back. No birds will ever use it again."

Uncle Martin let out a soft laugh. "Don't worry yourself, my pet. Robins always build a new nest. They never reuse old ones. It's yours to keep now. As a souvenir."

He placed the bowl of straw and dried mud in her hands. Its weight surprised her. When it had rested on the swaying branches, it had seemed so insubstantial. So fragile. She'd been startled to discover how sturdy it felt. Even so, when she'd prepared for her return trip to London, she'd carefully packed it to ensure it wouldn't be damaged during the long sea voyage.

Now she gazed at the bright celadon-blue bits of eggshell. Her bedroom walls perfectly matched their hue. To her, the color represented the indomitable spirit of life. Of home. Of happiness.

When she'd first married John, she'd created her own little robin's nest in their home in London. He'd balked at painting the walls celadon-blue, but she'd done her best to recreate the private retreat despite having walls the wrong color. Even so, she'd always known she'd eventually convince him to change his mind. She'd imagined her children visiting her there, laughing and romping as she readied herself for an evening's entertainment at some event in the city, or anticipating guests who would arrive soon for a dinner party.

And then a gun ended John's life. Their enormous house in London went to the new Earl of Harrington—John's younger brother. Josephine now lived in this smaller town home she'd inherited from her mother.

She'd never imagined she'd live here because she'd never considered the possibility that John might die at such a young age and leave her childless.

At least she could claim two annual stipends—one from the

Harrington estate and another from her father. She didn't live lavishly, but neither was life difficult.

Her situation might be a comfortable one, but she found the life of a widow to be stifling.

When she'd first relocated to this new residence, she'd tried to recreate the robin's-nest feel of the bedroom she'd shared with John. She'd even gone so far as to paint her bedroom walls in this particular shade of celadon blue. It hadn't taken long for her to realize she'd made a mistake. She couldn't recreate her former home any more than a robin could reuse an old nest. It was gone. The children she'd imagined would never exist.

There might be other children someday—another husband. She was young, after all. But immersing herself in a shrine to her dashed hopes and dreams made her feel as though she was trying to recreate a past that was gone forever.

Even so, she loved the color. It, at least, set this room apart from the one she'd shared with John. The color lifted her soul. Filled her with hope. She'd always been drawn to it. Always would be. It had been one of the things she'd first noticed about Frederick. Those celadon-blue eyes.

Up until recently, she'd imagined she and Frederick might— might what? Her entire body tensed as she thought of him. A week ago, the man had sent her heart fluttering and caused her cheeks to flush. Now anxiety and self-doubt replaced her tender feelings.

Was Frederick afraid of caring about any woman, or was it only her?

She'd thought better of him—believed their mutual attraction was more than a physical outlet for him. It certainly had been more for her. Much more.

Could a man separate his body and his emotions so easily? For her, what they'd shared only served to strengthen her feelings for him. It would appear he hadn't experienced the same response.

Frederick kept himself aloof. Last night's revealing interlude at

Lord and Lady Aldridge's perfectly illuminated their relationship, highlighting all the problems. Frederick didn't really trust her. He wanted her, yes, but not as his wife. Only as his plaything. That flash of jealousy might have proven he didn't want to share her with another man, but that wasn't enough. Not enough by far.

She knew he was attracted to her, but apparently his attraction wasn't strong enough to cause him to pursue her. It wasn't strong enough to goad him into laying claim to her and fighting for her.

She was worth more than that. She deserved more.

She refused to settle for less.

She would excise Frederick from her life. What other choice could she live with?

Pain seared through her. She'd come to care for Frederick, perhaps even love him. Why couldn't he love her too—love her enough to want to be with her?

❦

JOSEPHINE BREEZED BACK INTO HER TOWNHOUSE, BRINGING A gust of bitter cold with her. She'd ventured out to clear her head and let her decision settle in her mind. There was nothing like a brisk ride through the park to invigorate the body.

Well, almost nothing. Memories of that weekend with Frederick still haunted her. Waking up in her bed to find him still there, his arm flung across her as though claiming her in his sleep. The smile that curled over his lips when he woke to see her. The way he'd pulled her into his arms and buried his face in her neck, seeming to breathe her in. Their hurried kisses as he tried to force himself to leave her bed, wanting to protect her from discovery by the servants, yet unwilling to be separated from her.

Good sense had prevailed. Giving her one last hard kiss full of passion and promise, he'd slipped from her bedroom and back down the hall to his. She'd floated all day, and then they'd shared a second glorious night.

She'd returned to London walking on air. As each day had passed without Frederick, however, she'd dipped closer to earth. At first, she'd made excuses for him, thinking he might have been called away unexpectedly, but when no note, no explanation came, doubt began to seep in.

She'd finally resorted to contacting him, fool that she was. She'd told herself she wasn't pursuing him. She was simply worried he could be in danger. In her letter, she'd asked him if she should still expect him to escort her to the Koliada Ball at the Russian embassy.

His answer had been brief. He wouldn't attend.

But then she'd seen him there.

Even now, the memory both humiliated and infuriated her.

She detested lies. Detested secrets. She was a fool to be involved with a spy—a man whose entire life was a lie. She'd convinced herself he'd treat her differently from the way he treated the rest of the world. That she'd be with him inside his cocoon of trust rather than outside it along with everyone else.

She'd been woefully wrong.

Somehow, Frederick Woolsy had made her forget her ideals. How would she defend against him if her own heart betrayed her?

She needed to stand firm. He was the wrong man for her.

Determined in her mind, if not in her heart, Josephine hurried up to her room to change from her riding costume and back into a dress as blue as a robin's egg.

She needed to take control of her life again and stop letting things happen to her. *Carpe diem—seize the day.*

She refused to let her attraction to Frederick derail her and send her world crashing down. The wrong man was worse than no man at all.

It was best not to dwell on her decision, but instead to move forward and let other aspects of her life fill the aching void. After

John's death, she'd learned the importance of staying active and maintaining her other interests.

She pulled her lap desk from under her bed and placed it on a table while she settled onto the armchair near the fireplace. She draped a blanket over her lap. Domino approached Josephine's feet, tucked away beneath the throw, and plopped down onto them as she began purring noisily and kneading the soft blanket.

Josephine leaned over and scratched Domino's head before returning to her task. She arranged the small desk on her lap, extracted the small pot of ink, a pen, and some writing paper from the small drawer it contained, and started composing a letter. It didn't take long for her to pen her request to the curator of the museum.

After all, being a countess had its perquisites. Even a widowed countess wielded considerable influence in the British Museum. Especially one who had donated generously over the past few years. Mr. Beasley wouldn't be able to refuse her request to meet with him.

Josephine tucked the letter into an envelope and then let out a heavy sigh as she stared down at it. This was, truly, a delaying tactic. She'd put off the task that had been looming over her head long enough. She sent for her housekeeper.

Mrs. Drummer appeared in Josephine's open doorway a short time later. "Good afternoon, Lady Harrington."

"Good afternoon. I'd like you to prepare the supplies for Mr. Woolsy's poultice."

"I just finished gathering them together. Would you like me to deliver them to him?"

Josephine shook her head. "I'll take care of that. I plan to leave in ten minutes. Please arrange to have my carriage brought around."

"Of course," she said. She gave a curtsy and hurried from the room.

Josephine imagined being alone again with Frederick, and

hesitated. Maybe she should bring Mrs. Drummer along. What if Frederick tried to pull her into his arms again? Could she resist him? Could truly break things off with him?

She scowled at herself. She had to. And she didn't need Mrs. Drummer for added courage. Of course, she could always hope Frederick's brother Robert would be there to serve as a buffer.

Filled with resolve, Josephine lifted her chin. Seeing Frederick would be a test of her conviction, but she could do this.

She must do this.

✤ 9 ✤

"That went well," Lord Cary said as they began to descend the staircase in the Foreign Office.

"You think so?" Frederick shot him a hopeful look. He'd thought the same thing, but it was good to hear confirmation. "General Ratliff seemed more interested in the play he saw last night than in anything I had to say."

"Definitely." Lord Cary clapped him on the back as they clattered down the stairs on their way toward the main entrance. "Ratliff is always thinking about twenty things at once. The fact that he wasn't overly concerned with your credentials meant he was already familiar with them. With luck, you're well on the way to becoming the new spymaster."

"Now all I need to do is recover that church register." As he left the building, he tossed a casual wave over his shoulder to Lord Cary and immediately turned his attention to that troublesome task. It was still on his mind as he entered Woolsy House a short time later.

He immediately noticed something was different. The scent and sight of that difference struck him the moment he walked through the door. A large arrangement of flowers sat on the round table in the foyer. They might have a small flower conservatory here at Woolsy House, but neither he nor his brother or sister had bothered with this sort of display since their mother's death. It had been her domain.

Had his sister decided to try her hand at it? If so, she'd improved dramatically since her last attempt. The arrangement was stunning.

He pondered the mystery as he climbed the stairs toward his bedroom. Voices intruded. Robert's and—a stranger's. A woman's. Perhaps a new maid?

At the top of the stairs, he turned to find Robert and a young woman he didn't recognize standing outside his sister's bedroom.

Frederick narrowed his eyes. The pair gave the distinct impression he'd interrupted a tender moment. He could swear they were about to kiss.

There was something about the woman—something not quite right. In fact, if he wasn't mistaken, she was wearing one of his sister's dresses. "Well, isn't this a pretty scene?" he asked.

Robert jumped away from the girl as though he'd been scalded.

Frederick examined her closely. He and his brother traveled in the same social circles and knew the same people, yet he didn't know her. It was beyond coincidence that this particular stranger happened to match the description of the woman who'd stolen the church register from him at the Koliada Ball.

She had to be the thief.

"Frederick." Robert took a step toward him. "It's good to see you. I hope your meeting went well."

Frederick kept his gaze trained on the woman, and this seemed to make his brother nervous.

"This is our guest, Miss Antonia Winter." He glanced down at the woman. "Miss Winter, I'd like you to meet my brother, Mr. Woolsy."

Frederick examined her as she dropped into a graceful curtsy.

"She'll be staying with us for a few days, along with Lord and Lady Huntley. Lady Huntley has kindly consented to serve as chaperone."

My, but his brother had been busy. Was it possible he could have tracked down the thief, moved her into their home, and brought in a chaperone in such short a span of time? Maybe he was mistaken. Maybe this wasn't the thief.

He'd need to find out more about this woman. "Miss Winter? Now, where have I heard that name before?" Images flashed through his mind. Snatches of conversation. General Ratliff's ramblings. And then—"Ah, yes. Now I remember. You're the actress I've heard so much about."

"Am I?" she asked, startled but not embarrassed. "I hope it was nothing bad."

"Not at all," he said, trying to dredge up bits of what the general had said about her. "I hear you gave an outstanding performance in *Anne Blake* last night." He smiled at her, trying to get her to lower her guard. "Do we have you to thank for that stunning flower arrangement in the foyer?"

She blushed as she nodded, and Frederick relaxed. She'd be easy enough to question.

"Perhaps we should retire to the morning room," Robert said. "I only just arrived home, and I still need to speak to Landon to ensure rooms will be ready for our guests."

Perfect. Frederick grinned as he stepped forward and offered Miss Winter his arm. "Take your time. I'll keep Miss Winter occupied while you sort out the details."

When Robert's expression turned into a glower, Frederick's grin deepened. This woman was the thief. He was certain of it. But what game was his brother playing?

As he escorted Miss Winter down the staircase, he said, "I hope you don't mind my saying so, but your hair is a most unusual shade. It reminds me of a sunset on an overcast day." He shot his brother a smirk.

EVEN NOW, FREDERICK'S HEAD SWIRLED FROM HIS BROTHER'S revelations. Not only was Miss Winter the thief, just as he'd suspected, but she was also the granddaughter of a famous Russian artist. A painter. And she was now living in their house because the Russians had tried to kidnap her.

Apparently she wasn't "too important" to the Russians anymore. Not when they believed she had the church register.

How he'd allowed himself to become complicit in this mess, he'd never understand.

Or perhaps he did. He'd seen the way Robert looked at Antonia Winter. He was besotted.

Pathetic man.

Almost as pathetic as *he* was.

Frederick shook his head, still surprised he'd allowed himself to become enmeshed in this bizarre and untenable situation. But he'd had a strong motivation.

The book.

He'd been shocked when Antonia had agreed to help them. Apparently, she'd had no idea Queen Victoria hoped to use the book to avert a war. She'd stolen it because it held information concerning her family. She promised to turn it over to Frederick in exchange for being permitted to use it as evidence in a court case.

True to her word, she'd already retrieved the book. Now it was time for Frederick to follow through on his part of the bargain. The sooner Antonia stood before a judge, the sooner Frederick could give the church register to the Queen.

Frederick would have been willing to walk through fire to retrieve that book—he smirked at the thought as he flexed his hand. He certainly had been burned for it. And now the book was here, in the house. Fortunately, Antonia seemed to be a woman on the side of the angels. He could see why his brother was smitten with her.

Her barrister should be arriving later today. A Mr. Devin Montlake from Maidenhead. Yet one more house guest. Woolsy House was becoming quite the bohemian gathering spot. An actress, a barrister, a marquess, and a marchioness. Who would appear next?

Perhaps a countess.

He glanced at the clock on the mantel in the drawing room. Josephine had said she'd come by today with more supplies for his poultice. With luck, the diversion he and Daniel had planned wouldn't take too long. He should be back in plenty of time to see her.

Of course, with so many people in the house now, it was unlikely he'd have a moment alone with her. Even so, perhaps she'd come while the others were out.

He could hope.

Frederick was ready to put the plan into motion. He strode back into the foyer just as Daniel, the Marquess of Huntley, trotted down the main staircase, his broad grin in evidence.

Daniel and his wife would act as chaperones while Miss Winter remained in residence. The couple was approaching the situation as a pleasant diversion. An exciting adventure. He wasn't surprised by their attitudes. Not from such a bold and audacious pair.

Frederick nodded at Daniel. "Are you ready?"

"And looking forward to it." The man bounced once on his toes and then shot Frederick a broad grin. He'd changed in the past year. He was much happier and more relaxed these days. Marriage must agree with him.

Frederick ducked into the adjoining drawing room to peer out the window. He avoided touching the chocolate-brown curtains— he didn't want the men outside to notice them move and realize he was watching them as well. "They're still there," Frederick said as he returned to the foyer. "Five of them."

"With luck, they'll divide themselves evenly between us." Daniel shrugged into a heavy coat.

"Five doesn't divide evenly. Aren't you supposed to be good with numbers?"

Daniel stared at him flatly. "You know I'm only helping because you're Robert's brother, right?"

Frederick grinned as he put on his coat as well, but before he could reply, Robert and Miss Winter—or rather, Antonia— entered the foyer. "We're ready," Robert said.

"So are we." Frederick turned and gave Daniel a nod. "Once we're on our horses, you go left, I'll go right." He and Daniel would provide a diversion so Robert and Antonia could sneak away from the Russians and convince a judge to hear her case immediately.

Frederick scooped up the decoy package—a paper-wrapped box approximately the same size and shape as the church register.

Daniel gave a tense nod. "Meet you back here in thirty minutes?"

"Or however long it takes to shake the Russians," Frederick corrected. "Certainly no longer than an hour." He hoped. He didn't want to miss Josephine's visit. "Ready?"

Daniel grinned. "Always."

Frederick flung open the door. The two of them burst through it and bolted down the steps toward their waiting horses. As Frederick reached the pavement, he moved the small box from one hand to the other and intentionally dropped it as he tried to slip it inside his coat pocket. He scrambled to pick it up and surreptitiously watched as the five men shifted forward, becoming intensely interested in his performance.

Daniel seemed to vault into his saddle, but with Frederick's burned hand, he needed assistance from the groom.

Daniel paused, waiting for him. They needed to feign urgency, and Frederick realized Daniel's hesitation might look suspicious.

"Go!" he shouted. "Don't wait for me."

Daniel spun his horse around and sped down the street to the left. His sudden departure caught the watchers by surprise, but one immediately gave chase, tearing down the road after Daniel.

A couple of seconds later, Frederick grabbed the reins in his left hand and raced in the opposite direction, but that brief delay cost him. The remaining four men gave chase, and every one of them followed *him*.

At least no one remained behind to watch the house. They'd managed to draw away all five watchers, which meant Robert and Antonia would be able to slip away unseen.

Frederick's main goal was to draw his pursuers far away from Woolsy House, so he made sure he was an easy target to follow. He didn't want any of them to double back and catch Robert and Antonia.

He took a direct route toward Buckingham Palace. If the Russians believed he was delivering the church register to the Queen, it would keep them on his trail, if only to look for a way to steal it from him.

Carriages filled the streets, and Frederick maneuvered his horse between them while keeping his pursuers at a safe distance. After about ten minutes, he veered onto a side street and then turned down a row of mews.

The stables along the lane bustled with more activity than he'd expected. A carriage propped up on three wheels partially blocked his path. The coachman rolled a replacement wheel across the road, and Frederick sped past him.

"Careful there. Slow down," the coachman called out.

Frederick glanced back and spotted two of his pursuers entering the narrow road, but he couldn't find the other two. Had they lost his trail and split up, or were they trying to box him in?

Perhaps he was finally having a bit of luck and he'd lost them.

He could do with having luck work in his favor for a change. He was past due. That left only these two to deal with.

Frederick knew the neighborhood. As he passed Lord Saxon's home, he veered between two outbuildings and headed toward the main house, following a narrow path leading back to the main street.

When Frederick glanced back and didn't see any of his pursuers, he allowed himself to relax, just a little. At the next road he turned again. He swore aloud when he immediately spotted the first two men he'd thought he'd lost.

He tugged the reins, and his horse veered down a side street, hoping to avoid their notice, but it didn't work. He glanced back as the pair rounded the corner after him.

He'd made the blunder of heading in the direction of Westminster Palace again. Since that was where he'd initially been leading them, they'd been able to pick up his trail. He'd need to strike off in a completely different direction if he wanted to lose them.

Frederick dashed down another narrow road lined with well-kept stables. This particular road was quieter, and he was able to duck inside an open stable door.

A horse nickered a greeting, and Frederick's mount huffed in response. His horse was breathing hard, and Frederick let him move closer to a water trough and take a drink.

After a moment, Frederick guided his mount away from the trough. "You can have more soon," he murmured, "and an extra measure of oats too."

He waited a few minutes and then ventured back outside and peered down the mews. The stables still seemed quiet, and he saw no sign of his pursuers. He'd lost them.

LANDON, FREDERICK'S BUTLER, OPENED THE DOOR AND ushered Josephine inside the house.

Josephine came to an abrupt halt when she saw Robert and an attractive young woman were already standing in the foyer. They buttoned their coats as they prepared to leave.

"What a pleasant surprise," Robert said, looking genuinely delighted to see her. "I'm sorry I can't stay, but Miss Winter and I have an engagement."

"Well, fiddlesticks. I'd hoped to visit with you, too." She tamped down her disappointment. It would seem she'd be seeing Frederick alone after all. She hesitated as she looked at Robert's companion a bit more carefully. The young woman looked strikingly familiar.

"Lady Harrington, I'd like to introduce you to Antonia Winter."

As the young woman made a graceful curtsy, Josephine realized why she'd thought she looked familiar. Miss Winter was an actress. A smile spread across Josephine's face. "You're performing the lead role in *Anne Blake*, aren't you? I haven't seen it yet, but everyone says you're quite talented." But Josephine had the sense there was something more. She'd seen Miss Winter somewhere else recently.

"Thank you, my lady. You're very kind to say so."

She glanced from Robert to Miss Winter. Something here seemed odd. She could tell she was interrupting them. She turned her attention back to Robert. "How is Frederick today—or more specifically, how is his hand?"

"He's doing his best to ignore the pain. I believe he's out of supplies for the poultice."

"That's why I'm here." She lifted the small basket she carried. "I brought more leaves."

"He'll be relieved." He pulled out a pocket watch and glanced at it. "He left to run a quick errand, but he should return shortly. I hope you'll forgive us, but we have a pressing matter to deal with."

"By all means."

Robert turned to Landon. "Can you please show Lady Harrington to the drawing room and ask Frederick to join her there as soon as he returns?"

As Josephine followed Landon, she glanced back to see Robert usher Miss Winter through the door and noticed he placed his hand low on her back in a proprietary way. Josephine smiled in satisfaction. She'd been right. It would appear there was something between the pair. She'd suspected as much, although Robert had never been one to chase after performers.

It was an interesting development, but not surprising. Miss Winter's combination of beauty and talent must draw men to her. But something about the young woman—some memory—seemed to niggle at her. Had she seen her somewhere recently?

Josephine settled onto the sofa in the drawing room. About ten minutes later, she heard someone arrive. Frederick? No. That wasn't his voice. It was someone else. A moment later, the door flew open and the Marquess of Huntley strode into the room as if he owned it.

"Josephine!" he said, his voice booming in the quiet room. "Landon told me you'd stopped by. What a pleasant surprise. Frederick is out, but I expect him to be back shortly. He must have been delayed."

She tensed. The marquess always seemed a bit larger than life. If his reputation was to be believed, Daniel had a Midas touch when it came to matters of business. Of course, members of the loftier class publicly criticized him for sullying himself with such endeavors, but privately they were rather jealous of the man. It placed him in an odd position in society. For the most part, the overall opinion of Lord Huntley was that although he deigned to involve himself in business, he was somewhat redeemed by having the good taste to be ridiculously successful at it.

"Good afternoon, Daniel." She nodded toward her basket,

feeling she needed to offer an excuse for her presence. "I brought more supplies for Frederick's poultice."

"Ah! He'll be pleased, even if he doesn't tell you so. He was looking a bit ragged." Daniel crossed the room, tossing his hat and cloak carelessly on one of the chairs as he approached. "It's obvious he's pushing himself despite the pain. I've known Frederick since he was a boy. I don't think I've ever met a more hard-working and dedicated man."

Josephine felt pride begin to swell at his words, but she squelched it. The response had been an automatic one—and one she needed to eradicate. She managed a tight smile. "Surely he doesn't work any harder than you do."

Daniel gave a disparaging shrug. "It would seem marriage has tempered my drive." Then he held up his hand. "Don't misunderstand me. That's a good thing. It's better to have balance. Too much of anything is bad for a man."

"And for a woman too?" She raised a single eyebrow.

"Of course."

"It must be difficult for Frederick to find balance—given the sort of work he does."

Daniel narrowed his eyes, but said nothing.

"Don't worry. I already know he does work of a more—shall we say—sensitive nature?"

Some of Daniel's tension eased. "Sensitive. Yes, that would describe it well."

"Do you think he needs to find balance as well?" Hope fluttered in her heart, and she couldn't bear to swat it away.

"Perhaps, perhaps not. Frederick is different. I've never seen him give up on anything. Take the other night when he was burned at the ball. He convinced Robert to help him complete his mission. And even afterwards when he left to tend to his hand, he still stayed up half the night following a suspect through London."

She gave a gasp. "He did?" Blast the man. He'd pushed her out the door with the promise he'd go to sleep, but he hadn't.

He'd lied to her.

She hated being deceived, yes, but this particular lie—it pierced her much deeper than his others had. She'd revealed to him that she knew he was a spy, she'd proven to him that she could be relied upon, and yet he'd still lied to her.

When she'd first arrived, she'd doubted her ability to sever her relationship with Frederick. Now, resolve stiffened her spine.

She was done with him.

Daniel grinned, oblivious to her pain. "He's a determined one."

"Determined to get his own way, no matter what the cost." She didn't manage to keep the tartness from her voice.

Daniel's dark eyebrows drew together as he furrowed his brow. "Did I say something wrong?"

"No, not at all." She glanced at the clock on the mantel. "I just realized the time. Please pass on my regrets to Frederick and let him know I"—she cleared her throat as it suddenly became difficult to talk—"let him know I can't wait for him any longer."

Daniel peered at her closely. He seemed to know her words held a deeper import. "I'll let him know you delivered his supplies for the poultice," Daniel said as she swept toward the door.

"Do that. And tell him I said goodbye." Her stomach clenched as she turned and fled the room.

10

B y the time Frederick finally returned home two hours later, he was tired, he was frustrated, and his hands hurt like the blazes. But at least he knew he'd successfully distracted those men. They'd chased him all over the city.

"Good afternoon, my lord," Landon said as he took Frederick's hat and coat.

"Is Daniel here?"

"No, sir. Lord Huntley returned over an hour ago and waited for a while, hoping to see you, but he had to leave for an appointment. He—"

"Did he have any trouble?" Frederick peered into the drawing room. Had Josephine stopped by to deliver the poultice supplies while he'd been roaming around London? Had she left him another basket? He scanned the room. Nothing.

A sharp pang of disappointment speared him.

"No, sir." Landon pressed his lips together and scowled. "But another—"

"Send my valet to me." Frederick knew he was treating Landon abominably, but he was in too vile a mood to behave any other way at the moment. Once he had the pain under control, he'd be able to manage being civil. "I need his assistance immediately."

Landon's scowl deepened. "Very well, sir."

As Landon turned on his heel and stalked away, Frederick dropped onto the drawing room sofa. Herbert arrived moments later, carrying a small bundle.

"Can you scrape together any remaining bits of that poultice you made earlier today?"

Herbert nodded. "I don't know how effective it will be, but there's a small amount left." He handed Frederick the bundle, which turned out to be filled with ice. The man was a certifiable genius. Frederick cradled it in his hands and suppressed a moan of relief as the cold began to counteract the pain.

A few moments later, Herbert hurried back into the room carrying a cloth-covered bowl. Landon appeared immediately behind him.

"There's a gentleman here to see you. Mr. Devin Montlake, a barrister."

Was it so late in the day already? The lawyer must have traveled from Maidenhead in record time. "Send him in. I've been expecting him."

After receiving the letter, Mr. Montlake must have taken the very next train leaving for London. With a heavy sigh, Frederick sank back into the cushions of the garnet-colored sofa. At least the ice dulled his pain. Now he could think a bit more clearly.

Herbert sat next to him as he gently unwrapped the bandages from Frederick's right hand. Then he passed Frederick a bowl of vinegar-tinged water.

Frederick dipped his hand in a bowl and rinsed off the bits of smashed leaf. He lifted his dripping hand from the bowl and peered at his fingertips. How he'd managed not to break open any of those blisters was beyond him.

Herbert handed him a towel, and he blotted his hand dry just as his guest entered the room.

"Mr. Montlake. A pleasure to meet you. Please forgive me for not rising to greet you, but I suffered some burns the other night. My valet is helping me change the dressing. I wouldn't subject you to this if not for the urgency of our situation. I appreciate your making the journey on short notice."

Mr. Montlake's clear blue eyes pierced him with a gaze that seemed to take in every detail of his disheveled appearance. "Miss Winter sent for me. Is she here?"

"She'll be here shortly. She's meeting with Lord Tidmore to make arrangements for him to preside over her case now that she's acquired new evidence. Given the extreme urgency of the matter, I have every hope he'll hear it immediately."

The barrister raised his eyebrows. "That's excellent news. Her case troubles me more than any other I've dealt with."

"Have you known her long?" Frederick watched as Herbert gently applied the poultice to his burns. Although it didn't cause his pain to diminish as much as a freshly made poultice would, the effect was immediate. He leaned back against the sofa cushions.

"I'm fairly new to Maidenhead, but my wife, the Lady Cecilia, has known Miss Winter for years. My wife's father, Lord Babbage, owned the property we now live in, and Miss Winter lived nearby."

That caught Frederick's attention. "I heard Lord Babbage emigrated to France."

Mr. Montlake nodded. "For his wife's health. He wanted to take her away from England's damp weather."

As he recalled, Lady Babbage had contracted consumption. "Leaving one's homeland is a bold and drastic move. He must be a devoted husband. Has the change in location helped?" Frederick's valet gently wrapped a length of cotton bandage around the poultice.

Mr. Montlake nodded. "When my wife and I visited them in December, Lady Babbage looked much improved. My wife was greatly relieved to see her thus."

"Did they emigrate recently?"

"Yes. They moved shortly after our wedding, which was when my wife and I first took up residence in Maidenhead. I met Miss Winter's parents shortly before the tragic train accident that took their lives. When her uncle claimed her inheritance as his own, I served as the barrister for the Winter sisters. Everyone who knew them thought the court's decision in favor of her uncle was a grave miscarriage of justice, but the law was on Mr. Winter's side."

"We hope you can help us rectify that error." Frederick gave his valet a nod of dismissal. As the man cleaned up the poultice supplies and tucked them away in a basket, Frederick caught sight of the bit of celadon-blue cloth tucked inside. Josephine's favorite shade. He didn't catch a glimpse of the unusual color often, but when he did, he always thought of her.

Why hadn't she stopped by today as she'd promised? He'd advised her to have her housekeeper deliver the supplies. Had Josephine finally given up on him? The idea made his chest ache.

As he watched, Herbert tucked the blue cloth into the basket on top of the poultice-making supplies and then slipped from the room.

"Do you think there's a strong likelihood the judge will hear the case tomorrow?"

With reluctance, Frederick turned his attention back to Mr. Montlake and gathered up the threads of their conversation. "I'm certain he'll want to do so without delay. The church register is a complicating factor. Once the trial is complete, Miss Winter plans to surrender the book to the crown. The Queen will not be patient in this matter. If the judge agrees to hear the case, he'll need to make a decision within a day."

Mr. Montlake's eyebrows rose. "You *are* aware that's highly unusual, are you not? What judge would agree to that?"

"We have reason to believe Lord Tidmore can be persuaded."

Mr. Montlake nodded slowly. "I haven't appeared in his court, but his reputation precedes him. He might be the only judge who can do what you're suggesting."

"Then we must begin preparations immediately to go before him." Frederick rose to his feet. "Join me in my brother's study. You and I can examine the church register there while we wait for Miss Winter's return."

As he moved down the hallway toward the foyer, he thought he caught a glimpse of that shade of robin's egg blue again—Josephine—but it was just a glimmer of light reflected through one of the stained-glass window panels at the end of the corridor. He felt a pang of something. Disappointment that he hadn't seen her today? No. Not that. He didn't have time for that.

He showed Mr. Montlake to Robert's study, where the barrister quickly settled in. Mr. Montlake pulled out the notes and files he'd brought along and then glanced at Frederick. "Give me time to review these, then we can talk."

Frederick nodded and left. As he crossed through the foyer, the front door swung open. His brother and Antonia swept inside, bringing a cold winter wind with them.

"Good, you're back," Frederick said. "You'll be pleased to learn that Mr. Montlake arrived and is in the study preparing for court."

"That's excellent news," Robert said as he closed the door.

"Did Lord Tidmore agree to hear your case?" Frederick asked.

Antonia smiled broadly. "Yes. Tomorrow morning at nine."

"It's a good thing Mr. Montlake arrived promptly." Frederick rubbed at his chin. "Have you thought of anything else we need to do to prepare?"

Antonia frowned "Perhaps you can help me with a bothersome problem. I still need to prove my uncle was the man who stole the book from the Russian Orthodox church. The thief's hand was severely burned that night. You're a clever fellow. Can you think of a way to get my uncle to remove his gloves? He wears them all the time, and I need to know if he conceals his hands because he was burned."

Frederick nearly smiled. Gloves to hide burns. He was much too familiar with that concept.

Teasing out a solution to this problem would provide the perfect distraction from the thoughts of Josephine that continued to plague him. "You've given me an interesting challenge. Gloves, eh?" He considered the dilemma a moment longer and then gave her a curt nod. "Rest assured, I'll find a way."

Antonia's smile was full of relief, but Frederick barely noticed. He was already concentrating on this new puzzle. He just needed a quiet place to think.

No one would be in the plant conservatory now that evening was approaching. The gardeners would be done with their work, and it was unlikely anyone else would enter his mother's former domain. The spot would be perfect.

A heavy floral scent filled the warm room from the blossoms the gardeners managed to force into bloom in the dead of winter. Underlying it was the aroma of rich, dense decay rising from the soil.

He let the room's warmth and solitude envelop and soothe him, letting it work its spell, just as it always did, and drive away troubling thoughts.

But today, the room's magic shifted. Changed. Rather than peace, thoughts of Josephine filled his mind.

He imagined her smile—when that woman smiled, she smiled with her entire body. Her entire soul. There was no artifice in her. Every emotion was written clearly upon her face.

He paused, stroking the leaf of a nearby rosebush with the thumb and forefinger of his good hand. Actually, that wasn't entirely true. She wasn't open to everyone. She didn't divulge her thoughts and feelings to the world. Only when they'd been alone together had she truly revealed herself to him. Only when they'd spoken in private. Only when he'd slipped into her bedroom at the country house. Only when she'd given herself to him. When she was in public, her countenance displayed precisely what she wanted others to see.

She'd only let him see her, truly, those two nights they'd spent together. Let him see into her essence. He couldn't banish those images of her from his mind. They were seared into his very soul. Josephine with her lips parted as she leaned in to kiss him. Josephine as she smiled at him in delight. Josephine with her head tossed back in the throes of ecstasy—ecstasy he'd evoked in her.

Try as he might, he couldn't stand against those memories. He couldn't prevent them from surging into the forefront of his consciousness and distracting him. Having to exert so much effort to control his wayward thoughts was a new experience for him. Focus normally came to him as easily as breathing.

He pulled his hand away from the rosebush and accidentally brushed against a large thorn. It dug into his skin, catching on the back of his knuckle. He froze and carefully detached his hand from the plant before it could dig any deeper into him.

This was exactly what he'd been doing with Josephine this past week. Extracting her from his life.

He examined the spot and found a scratch, but the thorn hadn't drawn blood. The same couldn't be said for Josephine. When had she become an integral part of him? When had she invaded him so deeply that her absence now caused him pain?

He cupped his other hand—the more severely burned one. The fire had changed everything that night, leaving him distracted and careless. If not for his injuries, he would have noted Josephine's presence and successfully avoided her. Antonia would not have had the opportunity to steal the book. Everything would have been different.

But that hadn't been his fate. Instead, he'd offended Josephine, spurned her, and widened the gap between them.

He let out a heavy sigh. As the sun set over the homes surrounding Woolsy House, the vibrant colors of the conservatory's blooms faded.

In the darkening gloom, he had to face the truth. Josephine had taken his advice and decided not to deliver the poultice supplies.

He'd gotten what he'd asked for. She'd moved on.

So why did that leave him feeling so empty?

LATER THAT EVENING FOLLOWING DINNER, FREDERICK AND Mr. Montlake returned to Robert's study to continue working. They quickly became engrossed in translating the church register. Not only did Montlake want information from the pertinent page where Antonia's parents' wedding was recorded, but he also wanted some sample entries from other pages to check them for consistency.

"I want no surprises," Mr. Montlake said.

Despite the pain in Frederick's hand, he found himself completely immersed in the translation when Robert and Antonia entered the room. He glanced up from his spot behind Robert's desk, vaguely surprised by their arrival.

"How are the burns?" Robert asked as he crossed the room to stand in front of his desk. He looked relaxed and refreshed.

"Painful." He aimed an irritated glare at his brother. He struggled not to take Robert's smiling good humor as an insult. Frederick glanced down at the pen he held in his left hand. "A bit better, I suppose. I can manage to hold this in my off-hand." He tossed it on the table and flexed his fingers.

"Should I prepare the poultice again?" Robert asked.

Frederick shook his head. "All the herbs are gone. Lady Harrington must have finally taken me at my word and decided to stay away."

Antonia gave him a sharp glance. "That's odd. She arrived just as we were leaving for Lord Tidmore's house. She brought the poultice supplies with her."

Frederick stiffened. She'd been here? Why had no one told him? He shot his brother an accusatory gaze, but Robert seemed not to notice.

"Maybe she grew tired of waiting for you," his brother said. "I believe that was the gist of her complaint at the ball as well."

Frederick recalled Josephine's criticism two nights ago that he hadn't contacted her in days. He felt his face redden as he opened his mouth for a retort, but then Mr. Montlake pushed himself up from the seat next to him, interrupting him.

Devin Montlake shuffled some papers into a tidy stack. "I think the best way I can finish my preparations for tomorrow is to sleep for a few hours."

"Certainly." Frederick rose to his feet. "I'll direct you to your room. I could do with some rest as well."

Without saying another word to his brother, Frederick hurried from the study. After closing Mr. Montlake's door, Frederick continued on to his own room. He looked around. If Josephine truly had stopped by with poultice supplies—yes. He saw her basket now, sitting on his mahogany dressing table.

He crossed the room, flipped open the basket's lid, and found a cloth of robin's-egg blue draped over the contents. He nudged it aside with his finger and found the fresh poultice supplies nestled beneath.

He held the cloth gently, unaccountably pleased to know she'd come by as she'd promised. But she hadn't stayed, nor had she left a message. Why? Josephine did nothing without a reason.

Frederick rang for his valet.

When Herbert entered the room, Frederick gestured toward the basket. "Lady Harrington dropped off poultice supplies after all. Did you see her?"

Herbert looked surprised. "No, my lord. I'll ask the other servants. One of them must have put the basket in here."

"Please do, and find out if she left a message."

Herbert left, but he wasn't gone long.

"Did you learn anything?"

"Yes, sir. Lady Harrington was here earlier and met briefly with Lord Huntley. When he left, he asked one of the upstairs maids to leave the basket in your bedroom. She apologizes for not passing along the message that came with it."

Frederick's heart heaved. "A message?"

"Yes, sir. Lady Harrington said to tell you she was tired of waiting, and goodbye."

Frederick stiffened. "That's it? Nothing more?"

"Nothing more, sir. Perhaps Lord Huntley could provide a more detailed account."

Frederick let out a grunt. "Perhaps." A sense of overwhelming numbness consumed him. He turned his back on Herbert as he tried to process this information.

Goodbye? What did that mean?

A moment later, the sharp, fresh scent of crushed plants filled the room, piercing his momentarily dazed state. He glanced over his shoulder to see Herbert mashing the leaves for his poultice.

Frederick let out a heavy sigh and proceeded to shed his jacket and trousers. He wrapped himself in a robe and dropped into the chair next to the fireplace to let Herbert tend to his burns.

He willed his body to relax and let his valet's careful ministrations soothe him. Once Frederick washed away the remnants of the old poultice, he examined his fingertips. The raised blisters were much smaller, but the skin around them was still tender.

"Your hand appears to be improving." Herbert passed him a fresh cloth.

"Once I use up these supplies, I won't need to replace them." The thought left Frederick with a sharp pang of loss.

This wasn't what he wanted. He'd been fooling himself—trying to convince himself he didn't care about Josephine, even when a moment couldn't pass without him thinking of her.

Goodbye. The word pierced him.

He was obsessed with the woman. The look of her, the smell

of her, the taste of her. Her amazing blue eyes and her lustrous blond hair. He couldn't get enough of her.

Herbert put the supplies back in the basket and left. As soon as the door closed, Frederick sprang from his chair and began pacing the room.

It was ridiculous to think he could simply shut Josephine out of his life and continue on as before. Being with her had changed him, and he didn't want to go back to the way things had been before.

He stopped in front of the fireplace and braced the heels of his hands against the mantel, gazing down into the crackling flames.

He didn't want to live without her.

He pushed himself upright and spun around to face the room.

Enough. He'd come to a decision.

He wanted Josephine.

A heavy weight lifted from his shoulders. He could breathe again—for the first time in days. He threw his shoulders back and straightened his spine.

All it took was to make the *right* decision.

The next question was, how would he and Josephine meld their lives together?

If he became the new spymaster, he would be in London most of the time. His life would be more orderly. More conducive to being a husband. That would help tremendously. And with the church register in hand, the biggest obstacle to becoming spymaster was gone. But when it came to the issues preventing him and Josephine from being together, one significant problem still remained.

His father's secret.

In all good conscience, he couldn't continue to conceal it from her. He refused to put her at risk while selfishly indulging in his desire to have her—not when he wanted more from her. Not when he wanted *everything* from her.

It was time to take a chance. Time to be as open with Josephine as she'd been with him.

It was time to tell her about his father's treason.

⚜

THE NEXT MORNING, FREDERICK WOKE FILLED WITH RENEWED determination. In less than two hours, Antonia's case would be heard, and the moment they left the courtroom, he'd deliver the church register to Queen Victoria. Once he'd washed his hands of that mess, he'd head directly to see Josephine. He'd tell her about the changes he planned to make in his life—changes he hoped would bring them closer together. And he'd tell her about his father.

Yes—that was a solid plan.

He went to the breakfast room, his mind buzzing with millions of possibilities for how events might transpire. As was his habit when preparing for any mission, he ran through every foreseeable scenario, searching for potential problems. This was a delicate situation. He didn't want to manipulate Josephine, nor did he want to lose her.

Brisk footsteps approached the door of the breakfast room, and a moment later Robert appeared in the doorway. "We need to talk," Robert said as he strode forward. He paused and stood with his hand resting on the back of a chair, but didn't take a seat at the table. "I made a disturbing discovery last night." Robert stopped speaking and dragged his hand through his hair, leaving deep furrows.

Frederick tensed. Last night when he'd gone upstairs, he'd left Robert and Antonia alone with the church register. Had they made some new discovery?

Robert took a step toward the door as he beckoned Frederick. "Come to my study," he said curtly.

Frederick tossed his napkin on the table and followed his

brother. Upon entering the study, Robert turned back to brush past him and locked the door behind them. He paused, met Frederick's gaze, opened his mouth—but then stopped. "It's better if I show you," he muttered.

Frederick was surprised when his brother turned away, crossed to a bookcase, and began fiddling with something at the top of one shelf. With a click, the bookcase shifted ever so slightly. Robert gave it a yank, and the entire structure swung into the room.

"The staircase?" Frederick asked, stunned. Years ago, their younger sister Emily had discovered the disused hidden staircase and become fascinated with it, forever sneaking up and down the stairs so she could creep up on Father and surprise him. Their parents had finally blocked off the end leading to an upstairs bedroom by putting the bedstead in front of the concealed door. After Father's suicide here in the study, Mother had closed off the entire room. Frederick hadn't thought about the dark, narrow staircase in years.

Robert gestured toward a lamp on the table. "Bring that."

His curiosity piqued, Frederick did as directed. He turned back to find Robert applying something, probably oil, to the door's interior latch.

Robert glanced up at him. "Last night while I was searching for a place to hide the church register overnight, I realized this was the perfect spot." He gestured farther into the darkened space. "I was right. In all the years since Father's death, we never found what he hid here."

Frederick moved closer and spotted two bags—one of which was tipped over. Bundles of pound notes spilled around it onto the floor.

Frederick's breath caught in his throat. "The missing money?" He could hardly believe they'd found it in their own house— hidden here all along.

"This changes everything for us." Robert's voice seemed filled with hope. "I can finally compensate all the people Father swindled."

With a jolt, Frederick realized Robert was referring to his goal of secretly returning all the money people had invested—and lost—in Father's scheme. Frederick had always written off this particular obsession of Robert's as being nothing more than a way for him to salve his conscience. Seeing the relief on Robert's face made Frederick wonder if the need went deeper.

Frederick had never been particularly concerned about the investors' losses. They'd hoped to profit through no real work of their own by taking a shortcut. Frederick had never concerned himself with their financial ruin. They'd speculated on a decision by the House of Lords, and they'd lost. Things like that happened every day.

"Don't worry," Robert continued. "I'll make sure they don't know where the money came from. Since starting down this path a few years ago, I've grown adept at convincing people of their own good fortune."

Frederick let out a heavy sigh. "This doesn't resolve the key issue. With the evidence regarding the treason still missing, our family will never be safe. The Queen will never stop searching for her proof. Even now, the seal could have a catastrophic effect if it fell into the wrong hands."

A satisfied smile slid over Robert's face. "In that case, you'll be pleased to learn I found this as well."

As his brother picked up a small box, Frederick's heart gave a thud. "Is that what I think it is?" But it was. It had to be. He didn't need Robert's confirmation to know what his brother held.

"I'm giving it to you," Robert said, handing him the box. He stepped back, distancing himself from the object. "You're better suited to deal with it than I am. I'm confident you'll examine all the risks and choose the wisest path."

Frederick's hands were steady as he opened the box and peered inside. "You found it," he said, his voice barely audible.

"You decide what to do with it. I'll support whatever choice you make."

Frederick stared down at the Great Seal of the Realm. Or, at least, its exact duplicate. This wasn't the real one. This was the one his father had forged, using it to swindle so many people. Frederick always clung to the hope that his father's business partners had been the true criminals, but seeing the forged seal in his own house dashed those childish dreams. His father had been the true criminal all along.

Forging the Great Seal of the Realm was an act of treason. When Father's railroad swindle initially came to light, experts examined all the pertinent legal documents. Queen Victoria knew she hadn't applied her seal to them. She'd immediately realized they'd been forged. Father and his business associates had immediately fallen under suspicion. According to the facts Frederick had pieced together, Father had been on the verge of arrest when he'd committed suicide.

He stared down at the seal, weighing heavy in his hand. The decision regarding what he should do with it weighed even heavier in his heart.

Frederick considered his options. He didn't want to rush his decision. Too much was at stake. Between Lord Cary's retirement, his own possible promotion to the role of spymaster, his debacle concerning the church register, and the complications in his personal life, there was much to consider.

He was too close to this, he suddenly realized. He needed to discuss it with someone impartial. Someone who understood the ramifications.

He knew just the man. Lord Cary.

He tightened his grip on the box and then handed it back to his brother. Robert accepted it reluctantly, his face revealing his confusion.

Frederick held up a hand in a placating gesture. "I need to speak with someone about the situation and get his advice. Keep the box here for the time being. I'll seek him out after we leave court today. He'll be able to help me look at this clearly and determine the best course of action."

Robert was still for a moment, staring down at the box in his hand. "Do you believe in fate?" he finally asked. "Destiny?"

It struck Frederick as an oddly philosophical question, but then again, this was an unusual situation. "I believe people determine their own destinies. Fate is an excuse weak men use to explain away their own shortcomings."

Robert shook his head. "I used to agree with you, but from the moment I first noticed Antonia the night of the ball, even before we spoke, I sensed fate had brought her to me. I brushed it aside, but after she stole the book, I attributed that odd sensation to the theft. Now—what if this all happened for a reason? What if she came into my life to finally compel me to confront my past? She's been the driving force behind everything that's happened over the past few days. She made me care—made me become involved in something real. And now, if not for the fact that she wanted to hide that book, I never would have opened the door to the staircase and found this box."

A chill ran down Frederick's spine. He didn't like this talk of fate. Destiny. It went against everything he believed in. He relied on facts and details, not feelings and guesswork. He turned back toward the hidden door, and Robert stayed next to him. They pushed the door shut, hiding away the secrets once again.

Hadn't his thoughts wandered in the same direction as Robert's yesterday when he'd been in the conservatory? Hadn't he been wondering about Lord Percival's effect on his life? The fire had been caused by one small, careless movement, and it had changed his life.

No. He couldn't accept it. Life couldn't be that random.

"Coincidence," Frederick said, dismissing the idea with a sharp shake of his head. "You embraced the changes in your life because you were ready to move on, not because of fate."

Robert stared at him. "You've always said you don't believe in coincidence." He narrowed his eyes. "You can't have it both ways."

That irritated Frederick. He hated having his words thrown back at him. "You're a bad influence on me. Fate. Coincidence. Bah. Next you'll be talking about love."

Love? Where had that come from? He could feel the heat rising in his face as he turned his back on his brother and stalked from the room.

11

L ater that morning, Antonia's court case went according to plan. Mr. Montlake handled it masterfully. Everything transpired exactly as Frederick had anticipated.

Of course, she'd won. Preparation was key. That, and a preponderance of evidence.

As they left the courtroom, Frederick patted his brother on the back and congratulated Antonia. She was jubilant, as well she deserved to be.

Frederick couldn't help but notice that Robert and Antonia stayed close to one another. The backs of their hands frequently brushed together. Robert's need to touch her was almost palpable. It radiated from the man. The next time the couple's hands brushed, Robert's fingers twitched as though he had to force himself not to entwine them with hers.

Interesting. Something had changed between them overnight. Apparently, Lady Huntley didn't make a very good chaperone. After a single night under her supervision, Robert and Antonia had managed to move their relationship to a new level of intimacy.

Frederick took his brother by the arm. Robert left Antonia's side with obvious reluctance. Their relationship would bear watching, but for now Frederick needed to keep his mind clear. He needed to focus on deciding what to do with the forgery.

"Collect the book," Frederick murmured into his brother's ear. "Keep it safe. My meeting should take a couple of hours, and by then I'll know the best course to follow regarding the—other situation." He certainly didn't want to mention the forged Great Seal while standing just outside the door of Lord Tidmore's courtroom.

"Shouldn't the book take precedence?" Robert glanced around nervously.

Frederick weighed the risks. "I can't be in two places at once. The man I must confide in is leaving London today. If I don't speak to him now, I'll be forced to wait a fortnight for my next opportunity. I don't want the other matter to linger." He considered the problem for a moment and then moved closer to his brother. "Deliver the book to Queen Victoria without delay. Don't let her think we postponed it. Not even for a moment."

Frederick narrowed his eyes as he assessed his older brother. He liked the air of grim resolve he found.

Robert was up to the task. Of that, he had no doubt.

Frederick gave a sharp nod, turned, and hurried out the door.

⚜

FREDERICK QUICKLY TRAVERSED THE DISTANCE TO KING Charles Street. Luck was with him. Lord Cary was available when he arrived. For that, Frederick was thankful. If he hadn't been able to catch the man here, he'd have been forced to try to track him down at the Ambridge Club.

"It's good to see you." Lord Cary smiled broadly as he rose from his chair behind his desk. "Did you reach a decision regarding the position?"

Frederick took a moment to change the direction of his thoughts. Of course, Lord Cary referred to the role of spymaster.

"I have. My brother and I recovered the church register, which he's even now delivering to Queen Victoria. I'd be doing it myself if a new complication hadn't arisen."

Lord Cary's eyebrows rose high. "It must be serious indeed for you to place the book in his care once again."

Frederick didn't answer. Instead he moved closer to the large window overlooking King Charles Street. He pushed aside the gentle drape of the heavy gray velvet curtain. Below him, carriages, riders, and pedestrians hurried past. Everyone seemed intent on reaching their destination without delay. Wind tugged at hats and cloaks, encouraging people to be on their way. No one had any interest in what he said in this room, not now. But that would change if they had an inkling of what he was about to reveal.

He turned to face Lord Cary. "I'm sure you're aware of the scandal surrounding my father's death." He watched the man closely.

The spymaster nodded slowly. "More so than you might realize," he replied. He kept his gaze level as he regarded Frederick.

Frederick relaxes slightly. "I'm relieved to hear it." He took a step back and gathered his thoughts. After a moment, he glanced back up at Lord Cary again. "Can you explain what you already know so I can fill in the gaps? Be direct. Don't worry about offending me."

Lord Cary's mouth tightened and he gave a terse nod. "I know your father intentionally manipulated the House of Lords regarding a railroad deal." He watched Frederick closely, looking for a reaction, but Frederick kept his expression stoic. "The Queen suspects he and his business partners used a forgery of her Great Seal on his papers. The other two men denied any knowledge or involvement in the incident. Your father was on the verge of being arrested when he died. I suspect he knew this and chose to commit suicide instead. He left a letter naming a certain woman as his paramour, and he blamed her for his sudden despair. I never believed that particular story. I'm fairly certain she was either directly involved in the conspiracy, or she was blackmailing him—possibly both." He paused. "Am I telling you anything you don't already know?"

Frederick shook his head. "I'm here because of the forged Great Seal." He took a breath. "My brother discovered it last night."

Lord Cary stiffened in his chair. "Are you saying he actually found the forged item?"

"I held it in my hand this morning. It's real."

"What do you plan to do?"

Frederick tugged at his ear. "That's why I'm here. I'm too close to this. Too much depends upon making the right decision. I can't see a clear path through to the end, and I think it's because my fear is preventing me from thinking logically. I need your guidance."

Lord Cary leaned back in his chair and contemplated Frederick. "My guidance, eh? Well, my advice would depend upon what you hope to achieve. What's your biggest fear? What is it you most want to avoid?"

"Public humiliation." The words came out quickly, automatically. "For years I've been afraid that when the world found out my father committed treason, my family would be publicly reviled."

Lord Cary nodded. "Forging the Great Seal is treason, there's no doubt about it. Did you ever uncover anything that proves your father was directly involved in that part of the scheme? Any documents? Any testimony?"

Frederick paused. "I haven't yet thoroughly examined the cache of items my brother discovered. The Great Seal was in one of the traveling bags Father hid in our house." He recalled the way he'd fled from the room immediately following Robert's revelation. He should have taken the time to investigate the bags more carefully. Money had been spilled all over the chamber floor, but no papers. Could there be incriminating documents inside those traveling bags? Frederick shook his head. "I didn't see any, but I also failed to complete a thorough search. It's possible I missed something."

"That was careless, which is unlike you. You're obviously shaken by this."

"That's why I'm here. As I said, I'm not thinking clearly."

Lord Cary let out a heavy sigh. "The Queen has no desire for this story to resurface. It was a scandal fifteen years ago. One I'm sure she'd prefer not to revisit. In this, I believe your goals align with hers."

"Should I tell her? Hand over the Great Seal?"

Lord Cary steepled his fingers. "It's either that, or simply destroy it. We should consider that option as well."

"But if I destroy it, the question of my father's treason and the missing seal will never be resolved. It will always be a lingering question in the Queen's mind. If she never knows what became of the forgery, can she let the question go? Can she ever come to trust me as her spymaster if she always wonders if I might have the seal?"

"Do you hope to earn her confidence by turning it over to her?" Lord Cary rubbed his hands together and then interlaced his fingers. "Yes. I can see how that could work in your favor. You'd have much to gain if she sees you as trustworthy."

"My instincts tell me giving it to her is the best solution. Now that I've found the seal, I'd prefer to use it to close the books on my father's crimes. Once the truth is out, I'll be free of having to conceal them. I've hated shouldering that responsibility."

Lord Cary rose to his feet. "In that case, I suggest you deliver the item to her without delay. You say your brother found the forgery last night. The longer you wait, the more suspicious you'll appear if she learns about the timing. Resolve the matter immediately. If you turn it over on the heels of providing her with the church register, you'll look heroic. The perfect candidate for the spymaster position."

Frederick took a deep breath and let tension seep from his body as he exhaled. This was the path he'd tentatively decided upon. He'd been afraid he was letting his hopes for the future influence his decision, but Lord Cary's agreement put his mind at ease. "I can't thank you enough."

"No thanks necessary. Go. Clear your conscience." The corner of his mouth tugged up in a smile. "Confess your father's sins to the Queen."

❦

"What's this?" Josephine asked, glancing up as Taylor entered her office carrying a tray bearing a sealed envelope.

"I don't know, m'lady, but the man who delivered it said it was urgent. He's waiting for your reply."

Josephine frowned as she used a slender letter opener to slice the edge of the envelope and then extracted the single slip of paper. The note was brief.

Dear Lady Harrington,

I most humbly beg permission to call on you this afternoon. My thoughts are with you in this difficult time. It is my most heartfelt desire to be told that you are not too distressed to see me.

Yours sincerely,
Monsieur LeCompte

Distressed? What could the man possibly mean by that?

She sighed as she weighed her options. Allowing the notorious gossip in her house might be a mistake. What if his overly dramatic letter was simply a ploy to convince her to let him in so he could pry into her affairs?

But what if it wasn't?

She considered what the consequences might be if she rejected his request. A simple denial in itself was enough to elicit gossip if LeCompte manipulated the situation with skill. She glanced at the letter, that single word catching her eye again. *Distressed.* What if he started telling people that she refused to accept visitors? What if he offered speculation as to why? Had he learned of her tryst with Frederick? What if he offered up that tidbit for public consumption?

She tightened her grip on the letter opener. She couldn't take the risk. She'd allow him to call if only to find out what he knew— or what he merely suspected.

An hour later, Josephine sat in her drawing room, working on a piece of needlepoint she kept for just this sort of situation. She hated waiting with nothing to do, but she was too distracted to read right now and Monsieur LeCompte wasn't due to arrive for another fifteen minutes. She snipped off a length of bright pink floss and threaded her needle.

She'd had difficulty focusing on any task ever since leaving Frederick's house yesterday. She'd made the right decision to sever her relationship with him, but that didn't make her choice any easier to live with. Not when her heart was breaking. She poked her needle through the back of her fabric and drew it through with a broad sweep of her arm.

She might as well admit it to herself, even if not to him. She loved him. At least, she *had* loved him, for a time. Or perhaps she'd only loved the man she'd believed him to be, not the man he really was. Perhaps she'd only loved the phantom she'd conjured in her mind. The dream of what she'd believed him to be. Not the reality.

She couldn't seem to let go of that dream.

Reality could be immensely distasteful.

She took another careful stitch.

Promptly at three o'clock, she spotted Monsieur LeCompte's carriage depositing him in front of her townhouse. A gust nearly snatched away his top hat, but he caught it in time.

She tucked her needlepoint away in the small box on the end table and smoothed her blue skirts, brushing away a stray bit of the bright pink floss she'd been using.

From her vantage point in the drawing room, she watched as Monsieur LeCompte handed his coat and top hat to Fleet, her butler, and then swept his fingers through his dark thatch of hair. It obeyed him instantly, falling into place as though carefully arranged by his valet.

As he turned to face the drawing room entrance, he caught sight of her and stopped. He offered her a broad smile as he strode into the room. "Lady Harrington. What a pleasure to see you." His deep, resonant voice and pleasant French accent sent a pulse of awareness through her.

She dipped her head in response. "And you, Monsieur LeCompte. How kind of you to visit me on this blustery day."

"I'd hoped we might take a turn outside, but the weather—ah —it does not cooperate."

"May I offer a cup of tea to warm you?" She gestured toward the maid bringing in the tea tray. The girl placed it on the low table in front of Josephine and then left the room.

"*Oui, merci.*" He crossed the room and claimed the chair to Josephine's right.

Josephine carefully poured a cup of black tea, prepared it according to his preferences, and handed it to him.

LeCompte took a sip and smiled his approval. "Thank you. It's perfect."

She sipped from her own cup, watching him over the brim. "I must admit, monsieur, you piqued my curiosity with your request to call on me today. You mentioned my distress, but—well—for the life of me, I cannot understand why you think I'm distressed."

LeCompte kept his gaze level as one corner of his mouth tightened in a smile. "*Non?* Perhaps I read too much into the situation. I'm forever trying to put together the pieces of the puzzle, but sometimes I make mistakes."

"Am I a puzzle to you?"

He flashed his bright smile. "Aren't all women puzzles to men?" He set his teacup noiselessly on the saucer. "But in this instance, you happen to be a piece in a much larger puzzle. A bright spot of blue in an otherwise drab design."

She couldn't help smiling. "I can't imagine how I might play a part in a larger picture."

"Aren't we all playing our small parts in life? You, for instance. You quietly slip through society, free of so many of the restrictions placed on most women. You possess a level of independence seldom enjoyed by someone of your tender years. I doubt many are aware of how few limits are placed upon you."

She cocked her head to one side. "And why is my situation of such immense interest to you?"

He rolled his shoulders in a shrug. "You're a curiosity. Because of that, I've been watching you."

A chill ran down Josephine's spine. She didn't like the idea of anyone watching her, and LeCompte was more dangerous than most, given his penchant for gossip. She kept her face impassive. "That's a rather bold and intrusive thing to do, don't you think?"

"Not at all. I watch many people. It's quite interesting what one learns simply through observing others. You, for instance, seemed to be developing a strong attachment for Frederick Woolsy. That fascination seemed to be mutual. But about a week ago something changed—something came between you."

Josephine's teacup trembled in her hand, so she gently placed it on her saucer. "You're an observant man. I can't decide if I should applaud your skill or be terrified."

"Neither. I'm simply bringing a fact to your attention. I can't help wonder if Lord Cary is to blame for the increasing distance between you and Mr. Woolsy."

Josephine couldn't keep the confusion from showing on her face. What on earth did Lord Cary have to do with her? With Frederick? "I seem to recall seeing Lord Cary at Lord Aldridge's home the other night." She'd seen Frederick speaking with him too. She tried to recall any details about their encounter, but nothing came to mind. "What does Lord Cary have to do with Mr. Woolsy?"

Monsieur LeCompte was reaching for his teacup, but her words made him stop short for an instant. She almost missed that brief hesitation. As he lifted the cup, he gave a small shrug. "Perhaps not as much as I'd thought." He took a sip of his tea. "Do you plan to see Mr. Woolsy soon? I already know he and his brother are in court today, so you don't need to conceal it from me."

She looked at him blankly. "Why would they be in court?"

LeCompte furrowed his brow. "Apparently, I'm better informed regarding Mr. Woolsy's affairs than you are." He rubbed at his jaw. "I must admit, that gives me pause. After you left the Koliada Ball with him, I'd assumed the two of you had made steps to repair your relationship. Either I was mistaken, or you're excellent at dissembling. I doubt it's the latter."

Had he just accused her of being a bad liar? She was tempted to take offense, but she decided to let it go. "Is that why you came today? To question me about Frederick's movements?"

LeCompte shrugged. "He's been behaving quite oddly. Late meetings with Lord Cary, a court appearance, and his odd change in behavior toward you. I'd believed his attachment to you to be much stronger. I must admit, I'm confused."

Not as confused as she was. She almost blurted out that comment, but she managed to bite back the words. Is this how Monsieur LeCompte gathered his gossip? By startling people into accidentally revealing information they'd rather keep concealed?

He drummed his fingers against the edge of his teacup and then set it on his saucer with a clatter. "I saw something on the way here that troubled me greatly. I'd hoped you might shed some light on it, but now—"

She tensed. What had he seen? "Out with it, monsieur. You have been leading me throughout this entire conversation, and now you have me on tenterhooks. Has something happened to Frederick?"

He turned an oddly direct gaze on her. Gone was the flirtatious gossipmonger, and in his place was a man of deadly seriousness. "Not Frederick. It was his brother, Lord Wentworth. As I came here today, I witnessed him and a young lady in an altercation with a group of Russian soldiers." Josephine gasped, but he kept talking. "One of the men was on the ground between them, grievously injured and bleeding profusely. As Lord Wentworth and the woman turned to flee, a Russian darted forward and snatched a book from his hand. Lord Wentworth let it go and climbed into their carriage just as one of the soldiers tried to stop them. They barely managed to escape."

Josephine's blood ran cold. She hadn't understood most of what Monsieur LeCompte had told her today—Lord Cary, the court case... but this—this was different. Robert must have managed to recover the church register he and Frederick had lost the night of the Koliada Ball.

Recovered it only to lose it again.

"You say Robert and the woman escaped? Were they injured?"

Monsieur LeCompte shook his head. "Not that I saw. They appeared unscathed."

Relief swept through her. "Thank goodness." She felt a pang of sympathy for them for losing the book, but then stopped herself. She shouldn't care. She shouldn't let Frederick and his family steal their way back into her heart. This problem was none of her concern.

Frederick's many lies had made that abundantly clear. She wasn't a part of his trusted inner circle. She was an outsider.

She knew where she stood with him. He didn't want her in his life. He didn't want her involved with his work as a spy. He was a consummate liar. He kept her uninformed. He coddled her like a child.

Even LeCompte knew more about Frederick than she did.

She swallowed as she gathered her thoughts. "Witnessing such an assault must have been terrifying. I'm sure you were relieved to see them escape."

LeCompte watched her for a moment, judging her reaction. Making a decision. Finally he smiled, letting the role of the flighty gossipmonger overtake him again. "*Oui*. I wish I could have helped, but what was I to do? Alone? Outnumbered? I could only have made things worse."

"Of course," she said.

They chatted for a while about more trivial things. As Monsieur LeCompte left, Josephine clenched her fists so hard her nails bit crescents into her skin. She wanted to go to Frederick. She wanted to lend him her support.

But he wouldn't welcome it. He never had.

He never would.

So why did she feel her heart breaking?

12

Frederick arrived home a half hour after he left Lord Cary. Landon, grim-faced as usual, met him at the front door and took his hat and cloak.

Landon cleared his throat. "Lord Wentworth and Miss Winter are in the study. They asked that you join them the moment you arrived."

A knot of trepidation curled within Frederick. "They're here? Robert's meeting with Queen Victoria must have been brief. How long ago did they arrive?"

"Nearly an hour ago."

Frederick's knot of trepidation shifted and became a band of panic that tightened around his chest. Something had gone terribly wrong.

He rushed down the hallway and into the study. The moment he stepped through the door, he sensed the tension in the room. He tamped down his fears and presented them with a calm demeanor. "You're back early. Did everything go well with Queen Victoria?"

"We never saw her." Robert's voice seemed filled with sharp edges. "We never even reached Buckingham Palace. The Russians waylaid us right on the streets of London. The book is gone. Stolen. It's probably in the Russian embassy by now. Out of our reach."

"No!" This couldn't be happening. He stared at his brother blankly. He could hardly believe their carefully made plans had come tumbling down like a house of cards.

"We can recover the church register. I'm certain of it," Antonia insisted. "I know how we can sneak inside the embassy." She shot Robert a quelling glare. Apparently, they'd been arguing this point for a while. "If we go in tonight, we'll steal it from them before they arrange for a courier to take it out of the country."

"Your plan won't work," Robert said, obviously not for the first time. "It's ridiculous for us to climb up the side of the embassy on a rope and slip in through a window."

She stepped closer to Robert. "If we can gain access to the roof some other way, we won't need to climb up the side of the embassy. We could jump from roof to roof. The buildings are pressed close together in that area."

"Close, as in four to five feet?" Robert glowered at her. "That's hardly a simple jump."

Hope fluttered in Frederick's chest. Antonia might have the beginnings of a good plan. "I'm acquainted with the man who owns the house next door to the embassy. I'm certain he'll let us have access to his roof. Once we're up there, we'd only need to cross from his building to the embassy."

Robert shook his head and glared at Frederick. "We'd still need to lower ourselves to the upper windows of the embassy. That means you can't be one of the people on the roof." He glanced at Frederick's bandaged hand and then turned his glower on Antonia.

Frederick suddenly realized why his brother was so angry. "Antonia wants to be one of the people to break in?" He looked at her in stunned surprise.

"I've climbed many ropes before this in performances on

stage. I'm quite good at it. I'd originally planned to steal the church register using this same plan, but then I decided to slip in during the Koliada Ball. It was much simpler."

Robert turned to face her. "Just because you've climbed ropes in a theater doesn't mean you'll be able to do so four stories above the street. In the winter. With your hands in heavy gloves "

"Actually, heavy leather gloves should make things easier," Frederick said.

"You're not allowed to offer your opinion here," Robert snapped. "She's not going."

Frederick pushed between the pair and glared at his brother. "When you asked, I gave you leeway with Miss Winter. I didn't turn her in for treason, and I relied upon you both to deliver the book to the Queen. That should count for something. If you can come up with a better plan, then by all means, do so, but I don't see one. It will be dark in an hour. You and Antonia can break into the building under cover of night. Accept it, Robert. This is our best alternative. We can't risk letting that book leave the country in some diplomatic courier's bag."

⚜

FREDERICK, ROBERT, AND ANTONIA TOOK THE CARRIAGE TO the house adjacent to the Russian embassy. Turner joined them on horseback so he could guard the roof entrance of the neighbor's house. That footman was becoming more and more indispensable with each passing day.

Their plans were precise. Turner would secure the escape route and provide them with an alternative route if needed. Frederick would remain with the carriage and gather the supplies Robert would drop from the roof once he was finished with them, and Robert and Antonia would sneak into the embassy and steal the book.

It wasn't a foolproof plan, but Frederick couldn't think of a better one. He loathed having to impose on his brother again, but he had no other choice. It galled him that he couldn't steal the book himself, but if he became spymaster, this would be the first of many similar experiences he'd have. He'd need to become comfortable with orchestrating missions rather than conducting them.

"Good luck," Frederick said as the other two exited the carriage and joined him on the street.

With Turner's help, Robert lowered a long board from the roof of the carriage. Turner gathered some lengths of rope. He looped his arm through the center of each coil and placed them on his shoulder.

Frederick turned and caught sight of Antonia for the first time in her disguise as a young man. She'd already been in the carriage when he'd entered it, so he hadn't appreciated her full effect when dressed in men's garb. The transformation was startling.

She grinned at his bemused expression, tugged at her hat, and said in a cockney accent, "Thanks, gov'nor!"

Frederick shook his head at his own surprise. "You look completely convincing. I apologize for staring."

She just gave him a saucy grin and strutted toward the door of the house.

As the butler ushered Robert and Antonia through the entrance, Frederick climbed back into the carriage. The driver pulled around the corner to wait.

This was the worst part, but if he wanted to be spymaster, he'd need to grow used to waiting. His tension grew as the minutes ticked away with an agonizing sluggishness.

After an excruciating half hour, when the board Robert and Antonia had used to cross between the two buildings came clattering down to the street, along with a coiled rope, the noise made Frederick jump. He hit his head against the interior of the carriage, but he grinned broadly. He scrambled out, and in an instant, he and his coachman gathered the objects and stowed them on the roof of the carriage.

The coach took off a moment later. Just as it rocked to a halt in front of the house, Robert, Antonia, and Turner came rushing out the front door. Turner untied his horse from the back of the carriage, and Robert and Antonia scrambled inside with him.

Frederick grinned at the pair expectantly. After the silence dragged on too long, his smile faded as his stomach sank. "Well? Do you have it?"

He closed his eyes, not wanting to hear their answer. He already knew it.

Everything had gone wrong. They'd lost the book.

⚜

FREDERICK COLLAPSED ONTO HIS BED AN HOUR LATER.

They'd failed. Well, not entirely. Not exactly. Call this one a Pyrrhic victory. Yes, they'd recovered the book, but at what cost?

His hands still smelled of ash and smoke from handling the church register. The ruined church register. It had fallen into a fireplace and been burned. The book was completely unusable.

No one would ever learn its secrets.

The Queen couldn't use it to halt the imminent war between England and Russia.

Frederick shook his head. He needed a new plan. It seemed ludicrous to proceed with his original one. Not now. How could he report to Queen Victoria, give her the burned book, and then turn over the forged Great Seal? She'd want his head, and he'd be handing it to her on a platter. Perhaps he should offer her a shiny red apple to put in his mouth as a garnish. He grimaced at the gallows humor.

His plans were in ruins. His future in jeopardy. How could he possibly win Josephine back when he had nothing to offer her?

No security. No hope of a stable life together. Just a future as the wife of a spy who was the son of a traitor.

After this debacle, he might not even be a spy any longer.

Frederick flipped open Josephine's basket of poultice supplies and gazed down at the blue piece of fabric covering the contents. As he tightened his fist around the cloth, he realized the pain in his burns had eased considerably. He wouldn't need the poultice tonight.

Whiskey would work just as well.

A short glass of the amber stuff sat on a tray on his nightstand. Herbert must have placed it there. The man could always predict Frederick's moods, which was both astonishing and a bit disquieting.

Frederick dropped the piece of blue cloth on his pillow and snatched up the glass. He downed the liquid in one swallow, grimacing as it burned a path down his throat. He kicked off his low boots and dragged off his pants and shirt, tossing them on a chair.

When Frederick turned back to his bed, he picked up Josephine's bit of blue fabric and pulled down the covers, sliding between the cool sheets.

The scrap of cloth was soft in his hand. He laid it flat across his bare chest and smoothed it with his palm as he stared up at the ceiling. What would he do about Josephine? The Queen? The Great Seal? They were intertwined. He grabbed the corners of the blue square and draped it over his face. All he could see now was blue. Infinite blue. Josephine's blue.

He needed to focus. To think. He snatched the cloth from his face and tucked it under his pillow, out of sight.

The warmth of the whiskey wended its way through his body. He'd never had much of a head for the stuff, and even this single glass was ample to put him to sleep. He leaned forward and blew out the lamp next to his bed.

Sleep. A beautiful oblivion. Tomorrow he'd be able to see the solution. He'd step through it like a chess game.

Tomorrow.

◆◆◆

FREDERICK FLEW HIGH ABOVE LONDON. HE RECOGNIZED THE CITY below him. Once summer he'd climbed the 334 limestone stairs to the top of St. Stephen's clock tower to take in this view. The ascent had been a hot one, but well worth it.

Now, the streets below lay empty. The cold winter sky, dark and cloudy. He'd flown like this in his dreams before, but always in the daylight, never at night.

That darkness pressed down on him. Heavy. Dismal.

He dropped lower, hoping to catch sight of someone, anyone, through the many lighted windows below.

As he glided closer, the lights blinked out. Each time he thought he might catch sight of someone through an uncurtained window, the light winked off.

He dropped lower, flying toward the glow of a church. He'd find people there. Light. Solace. Comfort.

But the church doors slammed shut while he was still flying above the building. He circled it, flying lower and lower as he searched for another entrance.

A moment later, he realized he was descending too quickly.

He couldn't stop.

He crashed. But not onto the ground. Into it. The earth nearly swallowed him whole... but not quite. He found himself standing in a pit. An empty grave.

He gazed up at the starry sky from inside his deep hole, drawing solace from it, until the damp soil began falling down and filling in the opening he'd made.

He reached up, trying to push aside the dried leaves and soft earth, but the weight of it overwhelmed him.

He was lost to the world.

Buried alive.

His hand flailed, thrashed.

A moment later, a hand grasped his. Soft, but strong. It pulled, and despite the delicacy of its small, gentle tug, it lifted him out of the ground, plucking him from the soil as efficiently as a gardener's fist pulls forth a carrot.

He didn't emerge back into the churchyard. Instead, he was in a bedroom. His *bedroom.*

The earth below clung to his feet, trying to drag him back, and he lost his grip on the gentle hand. He grabbed at the solid bedpost, hauling himself up and onto the sheets.

But where was the hand?

He glanced around and caught sight of Josephine slipping from his room.

He called to her, but she didn't turn back.

She was gone.

Frederick looked down, and the pure white sheets on his bed changed before his eyes, becoming a soft shade of blue—celadon blue. Josephine's blue.

He moved to follow her, but something prevented him, holding him in place.

He was bound—tied to the bedpost. Tied with long strands of blue ribbon.

"Josephine," he called, but no one answered.

FREDERICK'S OWN VOICE WOKE HIM. AS HIS EYES FLICKERED open, he found his hand buried beneath his pillow, wrapped in the blue square of cloth.

Josephine.

Nothing else in his life would be right until he made things right with her. That much was finally obvious. Everything had gone wrong when he'd turned away from her.

It didn't matter what happened with the book. It didn't matter what Queen Victoria said or did. What mattered was Josephine. Being true to her. Being honest with her.

He'd needed to be on the verge of losing everything before he'd finally realized what was important.

He believed in her. If he took her hand, she'd never let him go. She'd always be there for him.

Had there ever been a bigger fool? He'd nearly let her slip through his fingers. Slip out of his life. He'd nearly lost sight of what was truly important.

Josephine.

13

J osephine stared down at the letter from Frederick in her hand. He wanted to meet with her. Today.

His timing was abysmal.

She shook her head decisively. She absolutely would not allow him to derail her plans. He couldn't assume he could waltz back into her life after abandoning her for a week and expect her to cancel her appointments. She'd scheduled a meeting with the museum curator for this afternoon, and she fully intended to keep it. Frederick's quixotic changes of mood would not alter her plans.

Men. They were perverse creatures. He'd finally gotten what he wanted from her—a cessation of all contact—and now he'd changed his mind.

She read the letter again. She had to admit, Frederick's request seemed heartfelt and sincere. Perhaps she should bend, but only slightly.

She sat at her writing desk and briefly penned a reply.

DEAR MR. WOOLSY,

It is with regret that I must inform you I have a conflicting appoint-

ment with a curator at the British Museum today at one o'clock. I am
therefore unable to meet with you at that time. I will be available
tomorrow afternoon and plan to receive visitors at home. Please feel free to
call on me at your convenience.

    Yours sincerely,
    Lady Harrington

SHE READ OVER THE BRIEF LETTER AND GAVE A SATISFIED NOD.
It would suffice. It struck the right note of formality and
politeness.

She sent the letter off with the eleven o'clock post.

৩৯৩

AT PRECISELY FIVE MINUTES BEFORE ONE O'CLOCK, JOSEPHINE'S
carriage drew to a halt in front of the British Museum. She
glanced down at Mr. Beasley's letter and read through the instructions for meeting with him in the vast building.

A moment later, she glided through the main doors and
located a uniformed clerk at the visitors' desk. She quickly introduced herself and asked to be escorted to the curator's office.

"Right this way, Lady Harrington," the man said. He hesitated
as he glanced over her shoulder. "Mr. Beasley didn't mention you'd
be bringing a guest."

Frederick's voice came from behind her, sending a flash of
awareness coursing through her. "I was a last-minute addition.
When I learned of Lady Harrington's plans for the day, I couldn't
resist the temptation to join her."

Josephine stiffened. She knew she should send him away. She
opened her mouth to do just that, but she couldn't force herself to
say the words. When he stood close to her this way, she couldn't
deny how much she still wanted him. How much she'd
missed him.

She glanced up at him, and when her eyes met his, the frisson of heat that passed between them made her catch her breath.

Frederick's jaw tightened, but that was the only indication that he'd felt the same sort of attraction she did. Of course, he'd have to be circumspect. They were at the British Museum, after all.

Perhaps seeing him in a public venue was for the best. If she found herself alone with him, she might not be able to resist the way he tugged at her heart.

The uniformed clerk gave a nod and turned to lead the way, completely missing the frown Josephine shot at Frederick. "You were supposed to call on me tomorrow," she whispered.

"Your letter said I should feel free to call on you at my convenience. This is convenient."

She let out an exasperated sigh. Trust Frederick to use her words against her. "I'll let you come, but you must promise you'll be on your best behavior. Mr. Beasley is a busy man. I was fortunate to schedule this meeting with him."

"On my honor," he said, holding up one hand. She couldn't help noticing that the gloves on his hands fit snugly. There were no bandages beneath them. Apparently his healing was progressing well.

He tucked her hand around his right elbow and hurried to keep pace with their escort. "What is Mr. Beasley's area of expertise?"

She tried to keep her gaze fixed on the back of the grayish-blue collar of their escort's livery, but she quickly failed and found herself staring at Frederick's profile. "Ancient Greece. He specializes in Lycia."

Frederick grinned and glanced down to meet her gaze. "I'm a bit weak on ancient Greece. Where is Lycia?"

Ah, how she loved that man's eyes. She swallowed before answering. "It's a region in southern Anatolia."

"Wouldn't that have been part of the Persian empire?"

She blinked up at him in surprise. "I thought you were unfamiliar with this particular subject."

His smile was slow, and only for her. He seemed to want to draw her into his world—to share his secrets. "I have an intense interest in the Persian and Ottoman empires."

She blushed. "An intense—" It was difficult to think clearly when he gazed at her that way. Was he saying he was interested in the topic because of her? But no... his work as a spy would require him to pay close attention to those empires. That must be what he meant. She cleared her throat. "Of course. Your work for the Qu—" She stopped herself and glanced at their escort. She'd nearly alluded to Frederick's role as a spy. She could hardly believe she could be so careless. He made her entirely too flustered.

He grinned, clearly relishing his ability to rattle her.

They descended the stairs behind their guide and followed him through a maze of corridors.

She cleared her throat again. "I'm here specifically to learn more about a relatively recent discovery. I'm interested in a particular Lycian tomb that a British archaeologist, Charles Fellows, unearthed in the early 1840s. The temple appears to be designed in the Greek style, but Mr. Fellows found it in Lycia. Experts from many fields are examining it. Mr. Beasley was generous enough to agree to meet with me today."

"Not my field of knowledge," Frederick said. He rubbed the back of his neck with his hand.

He seemed uncomfortable. Restless. Was it due to the confined space? "Perhaps the friezes of battle scenes from the temple will be of interest to you."

A moment later their guide stopped in front of a door and rapped sharply on the frame. "Lady Harrington and—" he paused and glanced at Frederick.

"Mr. Woolsy," Frederick said.

"—and Mr. Woolsy to see you."

The door swung open, and Josephine found herself facing a

man who was quite a bit younger than she'd expected. His skin held the healthy glow of a man who spent time outdoors, and he had an athletic build which led her to believe he wasn't purely an academic, but also spent time at archaeological sites.

When Mr. Beasley smiled and took her hand, Josephine sensed Frederick stiffen. Frederick flicked his gaze over the curator, blatantly assessing him, but Mr. Beasley seemed unaware.

"It's a pleasure to finally meet you, Lady Harrington," Mr. Beasley said. He glanced at Frederick with interest. "I hadn't realized you were bringing a guest."

Josephine introduced the two men. "Mr. Woolsy has an interest in the Persian and Ottoman empires."

"Oh," he said, his interest fading. "Not really my field of expertise, but given the location of the tomb, I'm sure you'll find this of some interest. I'm afraid I might not be able to help you regarding those empires. I know little about them. My specialty is in Greek antiquities."

"Was a cache of items from ancient Greece found in Lycia?" Frederick asked.

"What?" Mr. Beasley wrinkled his brow. "Of course not. I thought you knew. Mr. Fellows's discovery is an oddity. His monument is a place out of time. We think the structure dates from some 400 years after the nexus of Greek influence." As he talked, he turned his back on them and locked the door to his office. "The statuary and frescoes are astonishing. Mr. Fellows dismantled the entire monument and shipped it here to the British Museum. We're dedicating a permanent space where we can have it on display." He began walking down the corridor and waved for them to follow him. "Lady Harrington asked to see the statues of the Nereids and the notes from the archaeological excavation of the site."

Frederick glanced at her. "You mentioned you wanted to travel there. Is this why?"

She nodded, pleased that he'd remembered. "When do you

expect to have the exhibit open to the public?" she asked the curator.

"That won't be for quite some time. I doubt it will be before 1860. Perhaps not even until 1865, given the complexity of the task. One can't rush this sort of work."

Mr. Beasley pushed his way through a large door and into an enormous storage area. Josephine stopped momentarily, astonished by the immense size of the space. "Is this where you store museum items not currently on display?"

"Here, and in other locations around London. The pieces we're currently restoring or researching are kept close at hand for convenience." He gestured toward the rows upon rows of shelves. "We're constantly adding to the museum, and every item passes through this room."

He began making his way down a wide aisle, and Josephine hurried to keep up with him. "Are all the items from the monument stored here?"

"Yes. The location of our storage rooms makes examining them convenient." He paused at a cross-corridor in the storage area and turned left, then made a quick right. "Here we are."

Josephine stopped, stunned, facing a group of headless female statues, all wearing flowing gowns. "These are amazing," she said, her voice breathless. She moved closer, leaning in to examine one. "I heard that some believe Mr. Fellows's discovery is a monument to the Nereids since there are so many statues of them."

"That's one of the working theories."

"What are Nereids?" Frederick asked.

Mr. Beasley looked at him with surprise. "Oh, that's right. You aren't a Greek scholar. I'd nearly forgotten. Nereids are Greek water nymphs. Of course, that might be imposing too much Greek culture on a Lycian monument. As I'm sure you might guess, the monument is likely to be of Persian origin, but we simply don't know enough yet to declare that with complete certainty. But I digress. You asked about the Nereids. In Greek myth, they often accompany Poseidon and are reputed to come to the aid of sailors fighting storms."

Frederick cocked an eyebrow. "A sort of mermaid? But *not* a mermaid."

Josephine glanced at Frederick. "Unlike mermaids, Nereids symbolize everything that is good and kind about the sea. They're often depicted wearing white gowns and crowns of red coral, dancing about as they serve as Poseidon's escort."

Frederick glanced at the larger-than-life headless statue of a woman in a flowing gown. "And this is a Nereid?"

Josephine nodded as she stepped closer to Mr. Beasley to examine the neck of the statue. "It's a shame her head is missing."

"They were all missing when the monument was discovered," Mr. Beasley said. "Probably stolen long ago by locals. I assume they currently decorate some wealthy man's garden or dining hall."

"Such a shame," Josephine said, and patted Mr. Beasley's forearm. "It's good that people like you want to protect the monuments. Otherwise, they'd continue to be vandalized."

Mr. Beasley shrugged. "Some might consider Mr. Fellows the vandal since he took the entire monument. It's a shame he didn't take better notes before dismantling it."

Frederick stepped between Josephine and Mr. Beasley in what struck her as a decidedly possessive move, but Mr. Beasley seemed oblivious. "Do you have pieces of the frieze as well?" Frederick asked. "The battle scenes?"

Mr. Beasley nodded. "They're stored here." He indicated some wooden crates. He shifted a smaller box to one side and then opened a larger one sitting behind it. Once the lid was off, Josephine could only see packing material—sawdust and wood shavings. Mr. Beasley brushed it to one side to uncover the carved stone frieze.

"Oh, my." She reached out to touch the cold stone. "It's so detailed,"

"You'll note the man in the chair is dressed in the Persian style," Mr. Beasley said.

Josephine leaned closer to peer at the frieze. "The men standing in front of him appear to be wearing Greek style robes. I can see why this particular monument has brought so many researchers together."

A young man dressed in one of the museum's uniforms rushed toward them, a frantic look in his eyes. "Mr. Beasley, may I have a word with you? There's been an incident."

Josephine took a step back as Mr. Beasley rushed forward in alarm. In his haste, he tripped over the small heavy box he'd previously moved to one side. Frederick caught him by the elbow just in time to keep him from falling.

"Thank you. Thank you," Mr. Beasley said, clutching Frederick's shoulder as he caught his balance. "Would you excuse me for a few moments? If I'm not back by the time you're ready to leave, please don't feel you must wait for me. If you can't find he way, anyone here can help."

"Thank you, Mr. Beasley," Josephine said. "I'm sure we'll be fine."

He hurried off, in whispered conversation with the younger man.

Frederick reached out and touched the box holding the section of the frieze. "I'm glad I came with you today," he told her. "Seeing this has been eye-opening. I never really thought about the displays in the British Museum. They're more relevant than I'd realized. It helps keep things in perspective."

Josephine raised an eyebrow. "Relevant? How so?"

Frederick gestured toward a frieze panel depicting two soldiers putting a captive to death. "War and politics were as prevalent then as they are now."

Josephine stared at the frozen scene. "War has always been a part of life."

Frederick shook his head. "It doesn't have to be. A strong

society can stand against it. We have a stable government here in England. Our people live in safety and security. Our lands aren't at risk of being overrun. That's all because we have a strong government and a stable society. That's why it's important to defend the Crimean Peninsula against Russian incursion. If Czar Nicholas seizes control of the region, he's certain to restrict access to that waterway as well and prevent other nations from using it. That could deal a direct blow to the British economy."

She took a step closer to him. "Is that why you do what you do? Is that why you're a spy? Because you want to defend England?"

Frederick nodded. "I believe in our country. I believe in keeping it strong."

Pride filled her. "I admire that about you."

Some of Frederick's tension seemed to leave his shoulders. "I'm relieved to hear that." He moved closer. "There are some things I need to tell you. It's important to me that you know them. Hardly anyone outside my family does."

Her breath seemed to catch in her throat, and she hesitated before she spoke. "Then why tell me?"

"I trust you, and I need your guidance. Your advice."

His eyes locked with hers, and all she could do was nod.

"I haven't been fair to you these past two weeks. You're right. I was avoiding you at first. Not because I didn't care, but because I did."

She shook her head, confused. "That doesn't make sense."

"There's something you don't know about me. About my family. Something we've kept hidden for years. It has to do with my father."

"Your father?" That didn't make sense. "What does he have to do with us?"

Frederick let out a sigh. "Nothing. Everything. He's been dead for fifteen years, but his mistakes still haunt my family." He scrubbed his hand down his face. "There's no easy way to say this, so I'll simply tell you. Fifteen years ago, my father was on the verge of being arrested for treason. He committed suicide rather than face the shame."

Her jaw dropped and she covered her mouth, but Frederick barely seemed to notice. He just kept talking.

"Two nights ago, Robert found the evidence Queen Victoria has been searching for that proves our father was guilty. He showed it to me yesterday morning."

Josephine took a stumbling step backward and placed her gloved hand on one of the Nereids to keep from falling. "So, he's guilty? There's no doubt?"

"None."

"Did he turn over secrets to a foreign government?"

Frederick's eyes widened. "No. Nothing like that. Not that his crimes weren't bad enough. He forged the Great Seal of the Realm and used it to falsify documents and swindle investors."

Josephine took a deep breath and let it out slowly. It was bad, yes. Very bad. But it could have been so much worse.

Frederick ran his hand through his hair. "The Queen knew the documents were forged and immediately began searching for the culprit. Father was quite clever. He'd managed to distance himself from his original partners and made it appear as though they were the guilty parties. Everyone involved was questioned at length, but eventually the investigators began to focus their efforts on my father. He decided the only way out was to kill himself."

Josephine exhaled sharply. "That's terrible!" She pressed her fist to her mouth as she tried to compose herself. "I'm so sorry, Frederick. I'd heard rumors that your father had committed suicide, but I've never heard even a whisper of treason. You were so young when he died." She shook her head, bemused. "When did you learn about his crimes?"

"I found out a couple of years after he died. The truth came as a blow—like losing him all over again." Frederick shook his head. "In a way, ignorance really is bliss."

"I'm not certain I believe that. I suppose it depends on the nature of the lie—on its consequences. If it impacts me, I'd rather go through life knowing the truth than have it sprung upon me. It would be terrible to build your life upon a foundation of lies. Life isn't neat and pretty. It's messy and complicated. If we don't know the truth, we can't make good decisions."

"That's why I wanted to tell you about my father." He swept closer to her, taking both her hands in his. Her breath caught at the intensity of his gaze.

She tensed. Something important was about to happen. She'd need to keep her wits about her. She couldn't allow herself to submit to Frederick's charm. Not again.

He gripped her hands more firmly. "In all conscience, I couldn't pursue a deeper relationship with you without revealing this secret. It simply wouldn't be fair."

She felt her resolve weaken. "That's a noble attitude." The word caught on her tongue. Noble. That was Frederick. A noble liar. She tensed. She couldn't let herself ignore all the lies he told her. Not now. She pulled her fingers from his grasp. She couldn't put her heart at risk with this man. "What do you plan to do?"

He reached out for her hand again, but she stepped back. He looked crestfallen as he let his hands fall to his sides. "I don't know. My world has turned upside down. Not only do I need to reach a decision regarding this ghost from my past, but I also must consider the ramifications the situation with the church register will have."

"The church register?" Based on the tale Monsieur LeCompte had related yesterday, she was certain it had been stolen again. "What happened?"

"I have it now. We were able to recover it last night, only—" Frederick let out a sigh heavily laced with frustration and despair. "It's been damaged beyond repair. I can complete my mission and deliver the book to the Queen, but she won't be able to use it to negotiate a stop to the impending war with Russia."

Josephine placed her hand on his forearm and squeezed with a gentle, firm pressure. She couldn't take away his anguish, but she needed to lend him her support.

Frederick covered her hand with his. "I'm afraid that if I hand over both the ruined church register and the forged Great Seal at the same time, Queen Victoria will be furious. But if I hold back the Great Seal and she finds out I did so, she might lose faith in me." He shook his head in frustration. "I can't decide what to do."

She took in his weary features as he wrestled with his decision. "You've been living with your father's secret for a long time. It's obviously taken its toll on you." She paused and met his gaze. "Do you want my advice?"

He paused, and then pulled away from her, breaking their contact. After only a brief hesitation, he met her gaze and gave her a nod.

She looked into his eyes and tried to infuse him with the same confidence that now filled her. "I know how important honor is to you. You need to make the choice you can live with for the rest of your life."

He shook his head. "But it isn't only up to me. This needs to be a decision *you* can live with too. Don't you understand? If I hide this discovery from the Queen, you and I still have a chance to be together. The question is, could you stay with me and help me keep this secret, knowing that my father's treason might someday become a public scandal?"

Comprehension flooded Josephine. He wanted to hide his discovery from the Queen and never reveal he'd found the Great Seal—for her. So he could be with her. His actions now made so much more sense to her. All his lies. All his secrets. His father's shame had shaped his entire life. With every decision and in every moment, that long-held secret weighed upon him. It explained why he was so secretive. And why he turned to lies rather than truth.

Her chest was tight, but she fought to keep her voice gentle.

"Your father's secrets aren't causing the problems between us. They stem from *your* secrets. *Your* lies. This practice of deceit has poisoned you. Invaded your very essence." She looked into his confused eyes. "You lied to me the night of the Koliada Ball. You pushed me out the door and then you went to search for the thief. You lied to me because it was convenient, not to protect me. It was instinctive. The question is, what will *you* do, now that I've pointed this out to you? I need to be with a man who will be honest with me. I can't live a life where I don't know if I can trust what you tell me." She took a step away from him. "Unless you can change, I can't see a way forward for us."

He looked stunned.

"Unless you can be open and honest with me from this point forward, you need to forget about me and find someone else."

She turned on her heel and hurried away.

14

P ain ripped through Frederick's heart. He bolted after her, taking hold of her upper arm just before she reached the end of the narrow aisle.

She tried to pull away, but he held her gently but firmly in place.

She stared at his hand, then at him. "What is it? What more do you want?"

"Everything. Josephine—" He stared into her clear blue eyes. Her confused blue eyes. He moved closer, standing directly in front of her so she had to crane her head back to meet his gaze. "I want everything from you." He leaned closer, taking in her every feature and memorizing this moment. "I want you to look at me the way you did at Lord Saxon's house. I want to make you remember what we've shared. What we mean to each other."

He slid his hand around her waist, pulling her to him. She didn't resist. He bent closer, and her lips parted slightly as she stared at his mouth.

This was a woman who wanted to be kissed.

He swooped down and took what she offered. His wasn't a

tender kiss. Not a respectful kiss. His was a kiss suffused with the passion and desperation that coursed through him.

She responded. It was as though her own passion flared up to match his. As he devoured her mouth, she slid her hands up, burying them in his hair and holding him in place.

This was what he wanted. Craved. This woman. He needed her the way he needed air. He couldn't live without her.

Footsteps clattered in the distance—growing closer. They were moving fast. With a frustrated moan, Frederick broke away.

Josephine seemed dazed. She pressed her hand against her mouth, her eyes wide. It took a moment for her to regain a semblance of composure and slow her breathing. When she did, she scowled at him.

"What did you think you were doing?"

"Kissing you. Isn't that obvious?"

"I didn't give you my permission."

"I took your response as being tacit permission," he replied.

"It wasn't."

"My apologies."

She flattened her lips to a thin line and raked him with her gaze. "Fix your hair. It's all—" She waved her hands about. Hands that had recently been sliding through his hair.

Just as he finished smoothing it into place, Mr. Beasley came breezing into the narrow aisle. "Ah, you're still here."

"I was just leaving," Josephine said. "Perhaps you can escort me out. Mr. Woolsy will be along shortly. He has some thinking to do."

As she walked away, Josephine kept her back stiff and erect. She didn't even glance back as she disappeared around the corner.

He stared at the spot where she'd just been as a sense of loss swept over him.

He'd accepted the possibility she might reject him because of his father's treason. He'd even tried to prepare himself for the blow. But this?

Something deep within him fractured, creating a fissure that ruptured his very soul.

He'd never expected to face her complete and utter rejection of his morality.

That wasn't quite true. It wasn't his morality she had rejected. It was the way he'd hidden behind his father's secret and used it to justify his treatment of her. The way he'd distanced himself from her. It was the lies he'd told, over and over, to hide himself from her.

She was right. Lies were no basis for a relationship—for a marriage. They needed trust and truth between them.

The fissure within him widened.

They could have honesty between them. Surely they could. His lies were the only thing standing in the way. Not only the lies he told Josephine, but the ones he told himself as well.

He could change. He had that power.

Suddenly, he wanted truth with Josephine. He wanted it more than anything else. More than clearing his family name. More than his own dignity.

He glanced around him, taking in the rows of shelves containing ancient artifacts. All hiding their secrets. Their mysteries.

Did any of the artisans' secrets matter now, so many years later? Their greed, their petty misdeeds, or their enormous acts of treason? It was all gone. All done. All in the past.

He needed to let it all go as well. He couldn't change his own history. It was done. But he could change his future. His new goal in life could be to make decisions he could live with. Decisions based on honor, not fear.

And the first step would be to be honest with his queen.

TWO HOURS LATER, FREDERICK WAITED OUTSIDE QUEEN Victoria's receiving room. He'd thought his stomach would be roiling with apprehension, but instead, an unusual sense of calm had descended.

A few moments later, a diplomat pushed open the door of the receiving room and hurried through it. Based on the irritated glance the man shot toward Frederick, he assumed the Queen had dismissed him. Apparently, she was eager to hear Frederick's news.

A footman gestured for Frederick to enter, and he rose to his feet, gathering the items he'd brought with him.

Queen Victoria assessed him as he walked through the door. Frederick offered a low bow.

"You can leave us," Queen Victoria said to the footman.

The man silently closed the doors and left the comfortable room. Frederick had been here before, but as always he was surprised by the sense of welcome. This wasn't a space for intimidating visitors, but one that put them at their ease. He'd already come to the conclusion the effect was intentional. A space such as this would encourage visitors to let down their guard. Despite himself, he already felt it working its magic on him.

"Good afternoon, Mr. Woolsy. I trust all is well with you. I heard you were injured the night of the Koliada Ball."

"Thank you, Your Majesty. The burns are healing nicely. I'm no longer obliged to wear bandages."

She nodded. "That is good news, indeed." She focused her gaze on the parcels he carried. "What did you bring?"

"Two items I believe you'll find of interest, Your Majesty." He held up the rectangular package. "Here's the book you asked me to retrieve."

"Open it," she directed, gesturing toward a desk near a window.

He tucked the second package under his arm as he placed the first one on the desk and picked up a small pair of scissors. He snipped the twine wrapped around the paper and then used a delicate book knife to cut away the brown paper, revealing the blackened church register.

Queen Victoria raised an eyebrow, glancing at Frederick. "It's as bad as I'd feared after reading your report," she said. "Are its contents completely destroyed?"

"I'm afraid the pertinent pages are, yes. The book landed open in the fireplace. Other parts are largely unharmed, but the section pertaining to Czar Nicolas was destroyed."

She approached the book and carefully flipped it open, examining the blacked pages. "They're certainly unreadable." She closed the book, wrinkling her nose at the acrid smell of burned paper and leather. "How unfortunate. I'd hoped to be able to use this in my negotiations with Czar Nicholas. It would have been a gamble, though. The efficacy of my plan was questionable at best."

"I apologize for failing you," he said bluntly.

She waved her hand. "War in the Crimea is unavoidable. The Russians proved that point in the Battle of Sinop when their bloodthirsty admiral continued attacking those ships even after they'd surrendered. My people are angry about that senseless slaughter, as am I. Delaying a declaration of war isn't wise. If I'd acquired this book months ago, I might have used it to stop the war, but at this point, even if it were still intact, I doubt it could change what's to come."

"Thank you for telling me, Your Majesty. You've eased my conscience somewhat," Frederick admitted. "I'm not accustomed to failing."

She gave him a level stare, evaluating him. "I'm aware of that. You're a driven man. Intelligent. Hardworking. An excellent choice to become our new spymaster."

The words stunned him. "Your Majesty?"

She smiled. "Did you think the appointment of such an important position would escape my notice?"

"I hadn't thought the decision quite so imminent as to merit your interest."

"I met with Lord Cary yesterday, and he assured me you were his choice as a successor." Her expression revealed nothing.

Frederick tensed, tightening his grip on the package he still held. "In that case, Your Majesty, I think it's imperative that you take a moment to examine the contents of my second package." He held it out to her.

She hesitated briefly and then nodded, accepting it. She took a moment to weigh the parcel in her hands. "If this is what I think it is... it's such a small thing to have such far-reaching consequences. Just like that church register."

She'd guessed correctly, he suddenly realized. Somehow, she knew he'd given her the forgery. But how? Was it simply due to the size and shape of the package, or had Lord Cary told her?

She picked up a slim, ornate book knife from her desk and made quick work of the wrapping. As the paper peeled away, it revealed a small wooden box. She released the tiny catch on the side, flipped it open, and stared. Then she gave a small smile of satisfaction. "I've had people searching for this for fifteen years."

"My brother found a pair of satchels in a hidden section of our house," he said, "and this was in one. He turned it over to me immediately."

She slid a gloved finger over the raised lettering. "I haven't seen this particular design of my seal in two years. The true Great Seal wore out, and I commissioned a new version. The lines in the forgery are still sharp and crisp." She pulled it from the box, examining it closely. "I must admit, holding this is an enormous relief. I was always worried that some document bearing a forged Great Seal of the Realm would appear and cause trouble. At least that concern will no longer plague me." She smiled at Frederick.

"I'd expected you to be angry," he admitted.

"Because of your father's deeds?" She gave him a stern look, and Frederick suddenly felt like a child being reprimanded.

"Really, Mr. Woolsy. You're being most shortsighted. Why would I blame a loyal and hardworking subject for the wrongdoings committed by another? That's nonsensical. Surely you can see that."

He bent his head under her chastisement. "Yes, Your Majesty."

"You also proved your integrity and honesty. I value these traits." She lifted her chin, giving him a regal stare. "Congratulations, Mr. Woolsy. You're now my new spymaster."

⚜

EVENING APPROACHED AS JOSEPHINE USED HER BOOK KNIFE TO slice open the uncut pages of *A History of Anatolia*, taking care to make the cut straight and even. The action came naturally to her, and for a moment she wondered how many fresh pages she'd cut in her life. How many times had she been the first person to read a new book, carefully slicing open the edges of the folded paper to reveal the secrets hidden inside?

She turned to the first page, her greedy eyes eager to plunder it.

She barely noticed as Fleet, her butler, entered the room, and when he held out a silver tray bearing a single letter, she took it without glancing up.

She absently picked up her book knife and slid it under the letter's flap, slicing it cleanly along the edge. She flipped the envelope over as she extracted the missive, and only then did she recognize Frederick's handwriting.

She froze for a moment. Using her new book as a distraction, she'd finally managed to temporarily banish him from her mind, but now he was back. As insistent and impossible to ignore as ever.

That kiss. She shook her head. It had been intoxicating. She blushed to recall how quickly she'd become oblivious to her surroundings. She'd been on the verge of tugging off his jacket when he'd pulled away. What if he hadn't heard Mr. Beasley approaching? The thought of how close she'd come to being caught left her face hot with embarrassment.

She glanced down at the brief note and held her breath as she read it. By the end of the page, her chest felt tight. He was going to the Queen? She glanced at the clock on the mantel. He must already be there.

Had her words convinced him to go directly to the Queen? Suddenly, she couldn't seem to breathe. What if everything went wrong? What if Queen Victoria was furious with him? What if she dismissed him from her service? Frederick's work as a spy meant everything to him. She couldn't imagine him being happy doing anything else with his life.

She glanced at the clock again, but hardly any time had passed.

Worrying would do no good. She picked up her book again, hoping to immerse herself back in *A History of Anatolia*. Perhaps she could decipher the mystery of why a Grecian style monument had been found there.

She read the same paragraph at least four times. The people of the region originally spoke Greek until they were overrun by—by —She tossed the book to one side, unable to concentrate. How could she focus on the mystery of the monument when the mystery of Frederick was foremost in her mind?

Too bad she couldn't learn more about him by reading a book. Life would be much easier that way. "*The Mysteries of Frederick*," she muttered, glancing at her book in irritation.

Only Frederick could reveal himself to her, and that wasn't likely to happen.

She stood, brushing her hands down the front of her gown to smooth away the wrinkles that had formed while she'd been sitting.

She glanced out the window. The sun was just beginning to set, but the remaining bit of grayish-blue sky reminded her of

Frederick's eyes when he'd gazed at her in bed. When his pupils had grown large, banishing most of the color from them. A darker, grayish blue. A mysterious blue.

She tore her gaze away from the sky. She'd take a walk and clear her mind. She'd banish Frederick from her thoughts with a bit of physical activity.

She quickly donned her hat and coat and hurried outside. As she strode down the street, she was so intent on her goal that she nearly walked directly into the postman. He bobbed his head, sidestepped her, and walked directly to her door.

Fleet still stood framed in the open doorway. He must have seen the postman coming and had waited. The letter carrier handed her butler an envelope and then hurried on his way.

Josephine paused and stared at the letter in Fleet's hand. Could it be from Frederick?

She hurried back to her house and held out her hand to Fleet. As he passed her the envelope, she immediately recognized Frederick's handwriting. Her grip tightened on it. He must have already finished meeting with the Queen.

She ripped open the envelope, not worrying about clean edges and book knives.

The letter was short. Simple.

J.

It is with considerable relief that I report that my meeting with Her Highness was a success. She continues to hold me in high regard.

There is more news I would like to convey, but a letter will not suffice. Please inform me of a time when I might be permitted to call upon you.

Yours always,

F.

. . .

A CONFUSING MIX OF EMOTIONS WASHED THROUGH HER. Relief. Confusion. Excitement. But at the moment, relief won out. An enormous weight suddenly lifted from her shoulders. She felt five stone lighter as she tucked the letter into her coat pocket.

"Good news, ma'am?" Fleet asked.

She grinned. "Yes. Very good." She turned her back to her townhouse and continued on her way.

Frederick's new level of openness surprised her. Not only was he keeping her informed, but he also wanted to share some important news with her.

At first, she tried to ignore the flutter of pleasure he evoked, but then she gave in and allowed herself to enjoy it. She liked this change. She liked it immensely. But could she trust it? After all, he'd only sent her two brief letters. That was hardly enough to prove he'd truly changed.

But he was trying, wasn't he?

She stuffed her hand in her coat pocket and wrapped her fingers around the missive. It was best to view Frederick's letters as what they were: simple updates to a conversation they'd had when he'd asked for her advice. Nothing more.

Nothing to base a future upon.

She pulled the letter from her pocket and read though it again, hating herself even as she did so. There was no underlying subtext. Just a simple update regarding his meeting with the Queen. It was entirely circumspect and vague about the details. Of course, he couldn't very well mention his father's treason here. That would be lunacy. What if someone intercepted it?

She shook her head. Now she was thinking like a spy, too.

But there was that last part. He had more he wanted to tell her. And to do that, he wanted to call on her.

She frowned. She shouldn't let this man wheedle his way back into her heart so easily. She had to steel her heart against him.

She couldn't give in. Not now. Because if she was wrong and he hadn't changed, where would she find the strength to walk away again?

She brushed a gloved hand against her cheek, wiping away a tracing of tears.

Why did doing the right thing hurt so much? Better a small hurt now than a devastating one later, she assured herself. Because losing her heart to a man who could never open up to her would be a devastating sort of life. One that would leave her even more lonely than she felt right now.

❧ 15 ❧

The following evening, Frederick forced himself to remain motionless while Herbert trimmed his hair and shaved him.

He dressed with care, ensuring his evening clothes were brushed and in perfect order.

True, his appearance wouldn't be a deciding factor tonight. In fact, the way he looked would probably have no bearing on Josephine's decision. But he wouldn't take any chances. Not when so much was at stake.

Herbert used a brush to rid Fredrick's evening coat of stray traces of lint. He addressed every detail of Frederick's attire. Nothing escaped his notice.

The attention to minutiae served as a balm. Frederick's future depended upon tonight. He felt it in his bones. As things stood now, the current state of his life wasn't good enough. Not by half. Yes, he was the new spymaster, but the victory seemed hollow.

His heart held a gaping hole only Josephine could fill.

Frederick surveyed himself in the mirror, smoothing the line of his coat and noting the nearly invisible bulge in his pocket. No one else would ever spot it. He gave his reflection a brisk nod. "Good luck," he murmured. "You'll need it."

"Pardon?" Herbert said.

"Just talking to myself."

"Good luck then, sir. I hope all goes well for you."

Frederick locked eyes with him. "As do I. Thank you."

FREDERICK SAUNTERED INTO THE BALLROOM, KEEPING HIS EYE out for Josephine. She'd replied to his letter, informing him she preferred to meet him in a public setting. The annual Palmerton ball.

He scoured the dance floor and finally caught a glimpse of her as she spun past him in a waltz. Lord Temple held her in his arms. A bit too closely, by Frederick's reckoning. That man was becoming as irritating as a thorn.

It was no great task to watch them unobserved. Lord Temple smiled down at Josephine and then leaned closer to whisper something in her ear.

She smiled, but it was one of those polite smiles that didn't seem to reach her eyes. She looked a bit wan to Frederick. Strained. As though she hadn't slept well.

A sudden spike of jealousy stabbed him. He wanted to be the one holding her in his arms right now. The one whispering in her ear. He was certain that if it had been his voice whispering in her ear, her answering smile would have been more tender. More sincere.

The waltzers continued moving in a large circle as they traversed the dance floor. Frederick lost sight of her for a short time, but then he found her swirling toward him again.

Her eyes didn't gaze back at Lord Temple. Instead, they scanned the ballroom. As she moved closer, Frederick tensed, waiting.

Josephine's gaze slid past him, and then flew back.

Their eyes locked. She stiffened. Color rose in her cheeks as she glanced away.

She didn't look at him again, but neither did she continue to scan the room. She'd already found what she'd been looking for—or rather, who.

As the waltz ended, Frederick watched to see where they'd go. Josephine joined a group of her friends near one of the alcoves while Lord Temple escorted a new partner to the dance floor.

As Frederick approached, Lady Elizabeth caught sight of him and stiffened, moving closer to Josephine in a way that struck him as protective. She murmured something into Josephine's ear.

Interesting.

Josephine spun to face him, her smile tight and brittle. She appeared flushed as she touched her fingers to her face in a gesture he'd seen so many times before. It revealed exactly how nervous she was.

But it was her shuttered expression that made him feel as though he'd just plunged through ice.

She was closing him out. Keeping him at a distance.

How would he break through?

Honesty. That was what she wanted from him. That was what it would take. Complete honesty. But where could he begin?

"I've been thinking about you," he said, pitching his voice so only she could hear. "In fact, I've thought of little else since we last met."

Her flush deepened and she glanced at her friend. "Could you excuse us for a moment? I need to speak with Mr. Woolsy."

The look Lady Elizabeth sent his way was full of warning. "Are you certain that's what you want?" she asked Josephine.

"It's necessary." She gave her friend a confident smile as she took Frederick's arm. "Shall we walk?" she asked him. "I'm parched. Perhaps you can find something for me to drink."

"Certainly. I'm happy to do anything you want, as long as I do it with you." He slid his hand over hers, slipping his thumb beneath her palm to touch its sensitive center.

Her hand trembled. She blushed as she turned her face away from him.

They wove through the press of people. Frederick spied an open door leading into an empty corridor and aimed for it.

They slipped into the hallway. As a footman bearing a tray of drinks approached, Frederick moved to intercept him. The man paused so Frederick could select a glass of punch.

Frederick tilted his head toward a staircase leading to the viewing gallery. "Shall we watch the ball from above? The gallery provides a wonderful vantage point."

She nodded, and she lifted the hem of her skirts as they made their way upstairs.

Once they were there, he passed her the glass of punch. She accepted it as she approached the balustrade overlooking the ballroom. She took a sip and leaned her forearms on the railing, peering down at the guests. "Have you been up here before?"

"A number of times. I like watching people."

"I've noticed. You were watching me tonight while I danced with Lord Temple."

"You seemed distracted."

"Did I? Perhaps I was. I didn't sleep well last night, and I found my attention drifting."

"Was something bothering you—or perhaps some*one*?"

She studiously ignored him.

He moved closer, noting the way soft tendrils of her pale-blond hair brushed against the nape of her neck. He recalled kissing that spot. He also recalled the way she'd trembled at his touch. The need to kiss her there swept over him, and he had to swallow before he trusted his voice not to waver when he spoke. "Thank you for agreeing to meet me here tonight."

She sipped her drink. "I was relieved to hear the Queen was so understanding. It sounds as though she's aware of your loyalty.

I've always believed her to be a fair and level-headed monarch. Her treatment of you supports that opinion."

He watched her as she licked her lips. "I'd hoped you'd invite me to speak with you at your home."

She caught her bottom lip between her teeth. "I considered it, but decided not to. I don't trust myself alone with you. You and I are currently in a state of limbo, and I'm not sure where things stand between us. I thought I had severed our relationship yesterday at the museum, but then you sent those letters—" She shook her head in frustration. "Truly, Frederick, I can't continue on this way. Being with you is too painful."

He couldn't take his eyes off her. Everything she did was beautiful. Every movement was perfect. He knew he was hurting her, simply by being here, but he couldn't stop himself. He couldn't stay away.

He took a deep breath. "Josephine, I need you in my life. I realize that now, and I need to make you see it too. I need to make you want to be with me as much as I want to be with you."

"It isn't a matter of want. Many of the things I want aren't good for me. It's a matter of what's for the best. You'll destroy me, Frederick. Your lies and secrets will eat away at us. I'll never know if I can trust you. I can't live that way."

"I've been struggling to come up with a way to prove to you I'm determined to change. I might have become a secretive man in order to hide my family skeletons, but I promise not to be that way with you. Not anymore. Between us, there will only be truth and honesty. You have every right to expect it."

"I've expected the truth from you all along, but you've never given it. Why would that change? It's who you are. Frederick, you're a spy. Your life is based on lies and secrets."

"My brother once mentioned a quotation he used to guide his life. 'How few there are who have courage enough to own their faults, or resolution enough to mend them.'"

She furrowed her brow. "I've heard that before."

"Benjamin Franklin. He was full of clever bits of wisdom. I've pondered that particular line often, but always as it pertained to my father and his betrayal. Only last night did I come to realize those words applied to me as well." He took a deep breath. "I need to face my faults and take steps to mend them. I've reached a decision. If you want me to, I'll leave the Queen's service. You're right. My life as a spy is based on lies and secrets. I want to change. I want a life with you. A life you and I can share."

She stumbled away from him as though he'd struck her. "Leave the Queen's service? But Frederick, you can't. What you do means everything to you. It defines you."

"Being a spy doesn't mean as much to me as you do. I'd gladly give it up to make you happy."

Her mouth tightened and she pressed her lips together. "Perhaps you can say that now. Perhaps you could even convince yourself you were content for a while, but Frederick, that simply isn't you. You're clever and talented. Your brother says so too. Both he and Lord Huntley sing your praises. How can you give up something fundamental to who you are? Don't you see you'd grow to resent the sacrifice? I couldn't bear to think you would give up a part of yourself to please me." She shook her head vehemently. "I won't let you do it."

JOSEPHINE COULD FEEL HER HEART BREAKING. SHE COULDN'T let Frederick do this. She couldn't let him give up the one thing that meant the most to him. The one thing that defined him. Not in a mistaken belief that doing so would allow them to have a life together.

Despite the lies and the secrets, she loved who he was. She loved his integrity and his honor. She loved his loyalty and his intelligence. What outlet would he have for his talents if he stopped being a spy? She couldn't picture him doing anything else. It was too much a part of him.

"I can't let you give up what makes you *you* in a misguided attempt to heal *us*."

His brow furrowed. He plucked her punch glass from her hand and set it on a nearby table, then he took her elbows in his hands. He pulled her closer and gazed into her eyes. "I want you. I want you in my life. I want you to know my hopes and fears, and I want to know yours. I want my life to be an open book to you."

That sounded... sounded... wonderful. But even so—"Doesn't being a spy preclude that? I can't imagine that a spy would be permitted to reveal all his secrets to his wife."

His grip tightened on her arms. "Some wouldn't be mine to tell."

She thought about that, examining it from different angles. Finally she said, "I can accept the necessity of keeping someone else's secrets. The problem arises when you don't tell me how those secrets affect you. You can't keep me in the dark to 'protect' me. That isn't protection. It's manipulation, and I won't stand for it."

His expression softened. "What are you asking for, exactly?"

"To be your partner in life," she said in exasperation. She broke free of his grip and spread her hands wide. "To be your equal. To have you be honest with me and not put me off with some lie simply because it's more expedient than the truth."

"Like the night I was burned? The night I promised not to go out and try to track down the stolen book?"

"Exactly like that."

He nodded slowly. "In that case, I'd need a promise from you as well. Promise me you'll trust me when I say I must do something. Tell me you'll accept that I know my limits and am capable of weighing them against the urgency of the task. The trust you're asking for goes both ways."

That took her aback. He was accusing her of being overprotective. Was she? When she considered how she'd behaved the night of the Koliada Ball, she could see his point. She'd stepped in and tried to take over. She'd insisted. She'd pushed. She hadn't listened to his protests. Not really.

"I can try." But could she change? Could she let him put himself in danger? She wasn't sure. She let out a sigh. "We'll make mistakes, won't we? We'll break our promises to trust each other."

He nodded slowly. "Possibly. Probably. But we're only human. It will take time to change, but I'm convinced we're worth the effort."

She smiled, moving closer to him. "I don't want you to give up being a spy. I only want you to be honest with me. If we can trust each other, we can conquer anything."

He narrowed his eyes. "Are you aware of the demands of the life of a spy?"

"Are you referring to the last-minute trips? The broken plans? The dangerous situations? The times you disappear for days, even weeks on end?"

He gave a half-smile. "Apparently, you're well aware."

"How could I not be? I've witnessed it all for myself this past year." An idea came to her, and she cocked her head to one side. "Do you ever work as part of a team?"

"Sometimes. It depends on the assignment."

"Do you ever work with women?"

He paused. "Sometimes. If that troubles you, I can assure you there's never been any sort of romantic involvement—"

She gave a quick jerk of her head. "It isn't that. I was wondering if I might be able to accompany you. Perhaps I could start off slowly. Only go when you're certain there's no real danger. Once I've proven myself—"

He shook his head as though confused. "Are you saying you want to become a spy?"

She lifted her chin with a snap. "Why not? You already admitted you've worked with other women spies, and you know

I'd be good at it. I'm quite observant. I figured out your secret over a year ago. You might be surprised at my skill."

He narrowed his eyes, but she caught the glint of something devilish in them. He stepped closer, crowding her so she backed up against the gallery wall, out of sight of the ballroom below. "But you're a lady. A countess." He seemed to purr the words.

"And you're a spy," she said, placing her palm against his chest.

"I don't know any countesses who are spies."

She cocked an eyebrow at him. "Fiddlesticks. There's always a first. Women are doing all sorts of things these days. For heaven's sake, our monarch is a woman."

He wrapped his arm around her waist and pulled her closer. He tilted his head to one side as he leaned in closer to her. "The idea has merit," he murmured. "Of course, the best disguise while on a dangerous mission would be for us to pose as husband and wife. Who would ever suspect a married couple? But I'm not certain—"

Josephine suddenly felt lightheaded. "*Pose* as man and wife?"

"Unless you've relented."

"Relented?" The word came out more as a breathless sigh because Frederick took that moment to press his lips to the side of her neck.

"If you'd agree, then our marriage could be more than a pose," he murmured against her skin.

❧ 16 ❧

Frederick's heart pounded. The only sounds came from their heavy breathing, Josephine's gasps of pleasure, and —the noise of the ball taking place twenty feet below them.

He dragged his mouth away from the soft, tempting spot in the hollow of her collarbone. Her eyes fluttered open, but her gaze remained unfocused.

Frederick scanned the gallery for something, anything—and spied a door.

He grabbed Josephine's hand, shouldered his way through the door, and pulled her with him into the darkened room.

Once inside, he let go of her hand and took stock of his surroundings. In the light washing in from the gallery, he spotted a small table bearing an oil lamp, a box of matchsticks, and a Japanese cloisonné bowl containing a couple of spent matches.

He quickly struck a flame, touched it to the lamp, and tossed the smoldering stick into the bowl. He closed and locked the door, sealing them away from the Palmertons' ball and all their guests.

Josephine cocked one eyebrow at him and then glanced

around the room. "Did you have a sudden urge to riffle through Lady Palmerton's household office?"

Frederick glanced around, taking in the gilt-edged desk with its delicate chair, the oil portraits of children adorning the walls, and the comfortable-looking upholstered side chair. It was a pleasant space, filled with cherished items, and decidedly feminine. "The chair Lady Palmerton uses at her desk looks as though it would break under Lord Palmerton's weight."

Josephine's smile was sudden and charming. It brought a glow to her face. "I can't imagine him in this room. He's such a large man. He seems more suited to a battlefield."

Frederick crossed the ornate rug to put his hand on the desk as though testing it. He grinned as he turned and leaned back against it. "It's sturdier than it looks." He nodded approvingly as he glanced around the space. "I've changed my mind. Now that I think about it, I can easily picture Lord Palmerton in here. He'd overpower the space, but I have the feeling that large, upholstered chair over there is a favorite of his. It looks as though it was specifically added to this room for him."

She moved closer to him and slid her arms around his waist. "I'm happy we aren't keeping secrets anymore."

"You mean that *I'm* not keeping secrets." At this angle, with him sitting on the edge of the desk, they were almost eye-to-eye. He touched a loose strand of her pale-blond hair and then gently looped it around his finger, like a ring.

Her grin was impish. "In a word, yes."

He unwound his hand from her hair. It was hard to gather his thoughts when she was so close, so he leaned back slightly. "I have something else I need to tell you." When her hands tensed on his back, he shook his head briefly. "Not another secret. News. The news I mentioned in my letter." Her hands relaxed, and she began stroking his back. "I was approached regarding an opportunity earlier this week, and the Queen has already given her approval. I'd like to hear your opinion."

She tilted her head to one side. It was obvious he'd piqued her curiosity. "Tell me all about it."

"I currently report to our spymaster. He's been in that position since long before I joined the Queen's service." Suddenly restless, he pushed away from the desk and began pacing. "A couple of evenings ago, he told me he plans to retire." He stopped and met her gaze. "He wants me to take his place."

Josephine looked stunned. "But you're so young. Not that I don't think you're capable. Of course you are, but if the spymaster is retiring, doesn't that mean he's an older man?"

"I had the same reaction, but he says he's come to rely on my insights into the various missions he's managing. He says I'm the person best suited to replace him."

"And you're considering it?"

"Yes. It would mean I wouldn't travel as much as I do now. I'd need to be in London the majority of the time so I could easily communicate with my men."

Consternation furrowed her brow. "But you love what you do. Would you be content giving up being a spy? Wouldn't you miss going on missions?"

He shook his head. "I wouldn't give up missions entirely. Even Lord—" He stopped himself. "Even our current spymaster goes on them occasionally, and he doesn't particularly like doing so. I'm certain there will be more adventures in my future."

She gave an indulgent smile. "Apparently the name of the current spymaster is one of those secrets that isn't yours to share."

He tilted his head from side to side. "It's not something I mention in passing, but I'll tell you if you want to know."

She held up her hand. "I don't need to know right now. Perhaps I never will. You can keep that piece of information to yourself." She paused. "Are you telling me about this because you want my opinion?"

"Partly. And partly because I want to be more open with you. Do you think I should accept the position?"

"It sounds perfect for you. You're a master at chess. A strategic thinker. Being spymaster and planning the activities of an entire web of spies would suit you to perfection. I'm certain our country would be well served with you in that role. You'd also be based in London, wouldn't you? You already know that would please *me*."

"Then you approve of the idea?"

She paused. "Is it my place to approve or disapprove?"

He watched her closely. "You didn't respond to my comment earlier."

"Which one was that?"

"When we discussed going on a mission together—and I can assure you, we can do so quite easily once I'm spymaster—I mentioned that we'd need to pose as a married couple, or make it more than a mere pose."

"You're right. I didn't respond." She glanced toward the floor. "You asked my opinion on two important matters tonight. The first was whether you should give up your life as a spy for me, and the second concerned this new position as spymaster. I find your methods of imparting that information quite telling."

Frederick tensed. He didn't like the determined look on her face. This wasn't good. This wasn't good at all.

"You weren't being entirely honest with me. Not when you withheld your second piece of news until you knew how I felt about your leaving the Queen's service. I feel manipulated."

Frederick felt as though he'd stepped onto a weak spot in the ice. He'd known he needed to be careful, but he'd never foreseen this particular reaction.

It galled him. He prided himself on his ability to foresee problems and prepare for them. It was why he was so good at chess. It was why he believed he was suited to the role of spymaster. But Josephine had just proved to him that he wasn't nearly as good at this as he thought.

"I was trying to be more truthful with you," he finally said. "It looks as though I went about it the wrong way." He shook his head. "Maybe this change will be more difficult than I'd realized."

She looked oddly pleased by his confession. "It will take time. I don't expect you to change in one fell swoop. You've been secretive for many years. This will take some practice."

Practice—that meant—"Are you saying you're willing to keep trying?"

"Yes, Mr. Woolsy, I am. You're worth the effort." Her gaze raked his body. "I'm afraid you've left quite the impression on me."

He moved closer. Close enough to reach out and touch her. Close enough to feel the heat radiating off her skin. Close enough to catch the fresh scent of her hair. But he kept his hands to his sides.

"You've left a lasting impression on me, as well. I can hardly get you out of my mind. You're my last thought as I fall asleep at night, and the first one when I wake up in the morning, which is probably because you fill my dreams. You're never far from my mind. Every time I see a flash of blue, I think it's you. I love you, Josephine. I'll do anything to make you happy." A smile pulled at the corner of his mouth. "I'll even bring you on all my missions if that's what it will take to convince you I'm trustworthy."

As he spoke, he watched her reaction. Watched her surprise. Watched as her eyes filled with tears. Watched, but held back. Right now he wanted nothing more than to pull her into his arms. Kiss away the tears on her cheeks. Put a smile back on her face.

But instead, he waited. He wanted all that, yes. But he wanted more. Wanted it enough to wait for her to give it to him.

She opened her mouth wordlessly, as though too stunned to speak. "Frederick. Oh, Frederick." Her hand shook as she brushed away the silvery gleam on her cheek. "I love you too."

Frederick's hand slid into his pocket and closed around the item there. Pulling it out, he held it in the low lamplight so

Josephine could see the gleam of the celadon-blue stone on the ring.

"Then please, do me the honor of agreeing to marry me."

Josephine seemed to melt as she stared at the ring. "I—I don't know what to say. It's perfect."

"Say yes."

She ignored the ring, instead looking deep into his eyes. "Did you know your eyes are nearly the same color as that stone? I've often wondered about that. Was it a sign we were meant to be together? Because of that stunning blue of your eyes?" She took a shaky breath. "I was about to say that I'd love nothing more than to be your wife, but it isn't quite true. What I'd love more is to be the wife of a man I love who is honest with me. I'm hoping you'll be that man. I think you can be." She glanced at the ring again. "Can you accept a compromise?"

He tightened his grip on the band of metal and stone until it bit into his newly healed fingertips. "As long as you'll be my wife, I can live with anything."

"I propose a long engagement. Six months, to be precise. During that time, I'll accept your proposal and I'll be your fiancée, but six months from tonight we'll evaluate our progress. If we feel we've been truthful with each other, we'll move forward with the wedding. If not, we'll dissolve our engagement."

His stomach tensed. "Six months? That's a long time."

"But imagine the prize at the end of that time. A wedding. Us, together. And with the faith and confidence that our marriage will be strong."

"Will you wear my ring?"

She glanced at it. "Happily. I want the world to know we're together."

"Even Lord Temple?" he asked, grinning.

"Certainly Lord Temple. But I doubt he'll mind as much as you think he will."

He took her hand and slid it onto her finger. She lifted it, admiring the glittering gemstone in the lamplight. "It's perfect," she said. Joy radiated from her.

He couldn't stop himself. He pulled her into his arms, lifted her up, and spun around, twirling her in the air as he held her to his chest. "You're amazing. We're amazing."

She laughed and tossed her head back, squealing in surprise and delight.

He slowed, letting her slide down his chest until her lips were scant inches from his. He closed the distance in an instant, pressing his mouth to hers. Tasting the saltiness of her tears.

Her lips parted, and he plunged his tongue inside her mouth, savoring the sweet warmth within.

He moved back, leaning onto Lady Palmerton's gilt-trimmed desk and spreading his legs so Josephine could stand between them.

He wanted to slide his hand into her soft blond hair, and knock her hairpins awry, but he restrained himself. Instead, he pulled her to him again.

He'd been in this moment before with her—kissing her— worshiping her—but this time was different. This time he wanted more from her. He wanted everything she could give.

She let out a soft sigh of pleasure and slid her arms inside his evening coat, wrapping them around his waist. Her thumbs slid up and down the groove of his spine. She flattened her palms against his back and slid her fingertips beneath the waistband of his trousers. Teasing. Tempting.

When her fingers slid back out, she surprised him by moving to the fastenings of his trousers. She quickly undid them and slid her clever fingers inside. When she grazed the tip of his erection, he let out a groan. "Josephine, what are you doing?"

"Something I've been thinking about all week." She pushed his trousers farther down his hips and then wrapped her hand around him, sliding it up and down his length.

He let out another groan. "Woman, you'll be the death of me."

He pushed her away just an inch or two, leaned over, and lifted the hem of her bell-shaped skirt. Lord, how he loved these hoop skirts. The man who invented them was a certifiable genius.

Beneath the hoops she wore a pair of white linen bloomers held in place with a drawstring.

Frederick held her skirts in place with one hand as he tugged at the bow holding up her bloomers with the other. He quickly loosened it and they slid down her hips, pooling at her ankles.

He stared at her pale-blond triangle of hair. "I've dreamed of this. Of you." He reached out to touch her there, and she shifted closer, reaching her hand down to touch him as well.

He glanced up and found her staring into his eyes. Her face was soft with passion. As she stroked her hand from his base to his tip, his entire body trembled with his need for her. He wanted her, desperately.

He touched her soft curls, sliding exploring fingers between her folds. He found her liquid center, and he kept his eyes locked on hers as she let out a gasp of delight.

He quickly plunged one finger deep within her, and she let out a soft moan of pleasure. He glanced down, but her hoop skirts had dipped down and her soft mound of curls was now hidden from his sight.

He let out a groan of frustration and pushed her skirts to one side so he could watch what he was doing to her. Watch as he moved his hand inside her body. Watch as she thrust her hips rhythmically against him, whimpering in pleasure.

Her skirts slipped again, frustrating him. He needed to see her. Needed to touch her. Needed to be inside her.

He pushed himself away from the edge of the desk, grabbed Josephine by her hips, pushed her up to the edge of Lady Palmerton's desk, and bent her forward over it so her bottom was thrust into the air. He quickly lifted her skirts, draping the hoops over her waist, and was greeted by the sight of her bare bottom. Perfect. Round. Luscious.

Lord, she was exquisite.

He slid his hand between her thighs and used his foot to edge her feet apart, opening her more fully to him. He gently slid his hand into her soft folds, seeking her opening. He slid his first two fingers into her silken warmth.

"Frederick!" The word came out with a gasp of surprise. "What are you doing?"

"Giving you pleasure," he murmured, moving his fingers in and out of her, and then using her own slickness as he began making circles around her clitoris.

She let out another gasp and arched her back, lifting her bottom even higher.

His cock twitched in response.

He reached into the pocket of his jacket and extracted a French letter. He opened it and quickly slid the thin bit of protection over his eager flesh. She wasn't his. Not yet. The last thing either of them would want would be a pregnancy.

She trembled before him, open and wanting. He slowly, oh so slowly, moved his tip to her entrance. He held his breath as he pressed into her, savoring the warmth of her as her body wrapped around him. Accepting him. Welcoming him.

She whimpered as he filled her, inch by slow inch. She tried to press back against him in an effort to force him to move more quickly, but he held her hips firmly in place. He wanted this to last. He wanted to drive her to the brink of madness. He wanted to make sure she ached for him—yearned for him—for the pleasure he was about to give her.

This was bliss. This woman, this moment. He pressed into her, slowly filling her. He reached around her thigh to touch her soft curls, to slide his fingers into her folds. The moment he brushed against her hard nub, her entire body shuddered.

He began moving in and out of her warm sheath while simultaneously stroking gentle circles with his fingertips.

Her entire body shuddered again and again. She pressed her

hand against her mouth as she let out a hoarse sound, a stifled cry of passion. Between the muffled sounds and her spasming sheath, his own breath suddenly froze in his chest as he found his own release. He pounded into her in hard thrusts as his world exploded.

He shuddered, his breath now coming hard and fast. He leaned over her, bracing his hands on the desk on either side of her hips. He could feel her trembling against his chest, barely able to support her own weight after the all-consuming bliss of her orgasm.

Pure male pride filled him. He'd done this to her. He'd brought her to this point.

He reached back into his pocket again and extracted a crisp, fresh handkerchief. He was careful as he withdrew from her. He slid the French letter off and wrapped it in his handkerchief. He'd dispose of it at home. He wouldn't dare leave behind evidence of their tryst in Lady Palmerton's office. He neatly tucked everything away into his pocket.

He bent to gather the puddle of Josephine's pantaloons from the floor and raise them to her waist. Just before he pulled them over her hips, he paused, staring at her round, perfect bottom. He pressed a kiss just above the base of her spine and then pulled her pantaloons up the rest of the way. He made quick work of re-tying the drawstring.

He pulled down her hoop skirt, letting the fabric fall to her feet in a soft swoosh of satin.

She braced her hands against the desk and pressed herself upright. She turned to face him. Not a hair was out of place. She looked perfect. Untouched. The only telltale signs of what had just taken place were her slightly swollen lips and her dazed, satiated expression. One he was certain was reflected on his face.

A bemused smile spread across her lips. "Mr. Woolsy, I believe these next few months will be most pleasant ."

"I plan to make them so pleasant you'll never want to be parted from me."

The corners of her mouth turned up even more. "I have the same plan in mind for you. Finding precisely the right motivation can work wonders when it comes to making a change in one's life."

He moved closer, pressing his entire length against her as he took her hands and held them straight down to their sides. As he brushed his thumb against the gemstone that now rested on her finger, he locked gazes with her. "You're my motivation. Mind, soul, and body."

Then he wrapped her in his embrace for one last long, lingering kiss. She was soft and pliant as he pulled away from her. "A year from tonight, then?"

She blinked at him. "Hmm?"

He brushed the corner of her mouth with his thumb. "You'll give me your decision six months from tonight?"

She let out a soft, satisfied sigh. "Six months. I promise."

"Six months," he repeated. And not a day longer.

Six months later

The notes of the waltz ended, and the dancers took their time as they slowly strolled off the ballroom floor. Since the orchestra was taking a brief break, there was no need for them to hurry.

Josephine smoothed her hands down the front of her satin gown. It was the soft, fresh green of an English forest on a spring day. She'd given up wearing her signature blue color months ago, and she didn't miss it. If she ever wanted to catch a glimpse of it, all she had to do was look into Frederick's eyes. Those gorgeous, celadon-blue eyes that made her heart sing.

She was never far from his side, even here in Constantinople.

The British Embassy was crowded tonight. She glanced around, seeking out Frederick. Her gaze paused as a broad-shouldered man in black evening wear turned. She recognized him even before he faced her. The flash of his blue eyes sent a flutter of awareness through her. He was her home. Her center. Her everything.

The past six months had been exciting, filled with new experiences and new locales. Although Frederick was usually in London, she now accompanied him on all his missions. She'd finally had the opportunity to begin filling her curio cabinet with little mementos from their travels. The memory tied to each item was priceless. She loved waking up in the morning and peering at her ever-growing collection.

Frederick had proved true to his word. He'd worked every day to be truthful with her. He'd had a few problems with backsliding at first, but he'd kept trying. They'd both kept trying.

And they'd improved.

As he became more truthful, she was able to rely on him. To trust him.

Theirs was the relationship she'd always dreamed of. And to think she'd nearly abandoned it too soon.

"Lady Harrington," a man said as he approached her. "I received a letter from Mr. Beasley at the British Museum informing me you were passing through Constantinople on your way to Lycia. I'm delighted to welcome you."

Josephine took in the tall, slim, anemic-looking academic. "What a pleasure to see you again, Mr. Rahim. I recall meeting you earlier this year at the British Museum."

"Ah, yes. And how is Mr. Beasley?"

"He's quite well. He's busy working on the Nereid monument. I've been looking forward to this trip for months. I find it impossible to resist visiting the site in Lycia where Mr. Fellows uncovered the monument. For a researcher, there's nothing better than direct, firsthand knowledge."

"I envy you," he replied. "I doubt my constitution would countenance such an arduous trip. But you're a vision of health. Just remember to wear sturdy shoes. Don't risk twisting an ankle." He gave a small shudder. "Or blisters. Blisters can be quite troublesome."

"Sturdy shoes. Thank you for your excellent advice, Mr.

Rahim. I'll be sure to follow it." She glanced away to hide the mirth in her eyes and caught sight of Frederick moving toward them.

"I hear there's even more to your trip than a visit to examine some old ruins," Mr. Rahim commented.

Josephine tensed as a flutter of apprehension ran through her. Could he know about their mission? Surely not. That didn't make sense. She relaxed and gave him a teasing smile. "Really? I hope the rumors aren't scandalous. I'd hate to have my reputation in tatters."

The man chortled. "Perish the thought. No, I'm referring to your research. Rumor has it you believe you've discovered some enormous secret regarding the tomb and are here to confirm it."

Josephine frowned in surprise. "Mr. Rahim. You astound me. I wasn't aware my research was common knowledge."

"Oh, oh, my," Mr. Rahim sputtered, looking enormously flustered, "I do beg your pardon. I hope I haven't offended you."

"Certainly not. I'm flattered you've been following my work so closely." But this served as a warning she'd need to guard her research more carefully in the future. It would be horrifying if some other researcher swooped in and wrote her paper before she could.

Mr. Rahim glanced over her shoulder, and Josephine was surprised to discover that his already too-pale skin could turn even whiter. "I—Your—Please forgive me, but is your fiancé as understanding as you are?"

Josephine turned as Frederick arrived and rested his palm on her waist, just above the swell of her hoop skirts. She loved that possessive gesture. It made her feel as though she belonged here. That they belonged together. It also sent a shiver of awareness through her.

"Frederick, I'd like to introduce you to Mr. Azize Rahim. He's a researcher I met in London. He mentioned he'd heard I was coming to Constantinople."

She glanced up at Frederick, and understanding flashed between them. The excuse they'd given for their visit to Anatolia had been picked up and spread about. That would make tonight's mission much easier.

"It's a pleasure to make your acquaintance, Mr. Rahim. Lady Harrington frequently discusses both her research and that of her colleagues with me. She's mentioned your work in Lycia."

The man's face flushed slightly, adding needed color to those pale cheeks. "It's been too long since I've been able to go there. My health—well, I've suffered a decline. I've been following Lady Harrington's work with great interest. I'm looking forward to reading all about her new discoveries and theories after she visits Lycia. I believe she's the only woman who is currently undertaking such investigations."

"Surely not," Josephine protested. "In fact, I read something recently by Mrs. Westport. She provided fascinating insight into the daily habits of the population living in the region back in 640."

"Really? I must have missed that. I'll look into it."

"You should. Her work is excellent."

The orchestra's violinist began playing a few lilting notes, and after a measure, the rest of the orchestra joined in. She loved this particular waltz, and she couldn't help but smile in anticipation.

"I hope you'll excuse us, Mr. Rahim," Frederick said, "but Josephine promised this waltz to me."

"But of course," he said, gesturing them toward the dance floor.

Frederick swept her into his arms and they began twirling around the ballroom.

Josephine tipped her head back for a moment, allowing the glittering chandeliers and bright fabrics of the women's gowns to create a kaleidoscope of color as she spun about. When she refocused her gaze on Frederick's blue eyes, she was delighted by the love she saw in them. She melted inside.

Tonight. This was the night. They both knew it. She licked her lips. They still had a mission to complete. Waiting to give him his answer until after they were done felt like tempting fate, and she was never one to court bad luck during a mission. Waiting felt unlucky. She could feel it deep in her core. She'd tell him now. Right here on the ballroom floor.

His eyes glittered under the embassy's chandeliers. "You're glorious tonight. Did I mention that earlier?"

"No," she said, grinning, "but I believe you mentioned the word 'intoxicating' when you interrupted me as I was dressing for the evening. You nearly disrupted our timetable with your mischief."

He waggled his eyebrows. "I live to be mischievous with you. You're my undoing, my dear. I've learned to anticipate your impact on me and plan for it."

She nearly lost her composure. "Do you mean to say you included bedding me in your schedule for tonight?" She scowled in mock severity. "Does that mean I'm becoming too predictable?"

"Predictably intoxicating? That's a good thing." He tightened his arm about her waist, pulling her closer for a moment. "Too bad we have a schedule to keep. I'd love nothing more than to pull you into one of those alcoves and make love to you until you're trembling under my kisses."

Her breath caught in her throat. "You wouldn't."

Frederick leaned closer, murmuring in her ear. "I would, if not for the fact that we have a tight schedule tonight." The warmth of his breath brushing against her ear sent a shiver down her spine.

She exhaled shakily. "Just like every night when we're on a mission. You always plan things to the last second."

"Can I help it that I'm a stickler for details?"

"I wouldn't have you any other way. It's gotten us out of a difficult situation more times than I like to recall."

He cocked his head to one side as he gazed into her eyes.

"Speaking of being a stickler for details, do you happen to remember what day it is today?"

She couldn't hold back her smile. She'd been waiting for this moment. "How could I not? Isn't that why you arranged everything so we'd be here tonight? Constantinople is decidedly romantic."

He grinned back at her. "I wanted to make certain you were in the right frame of mind."

She grinned at that. "You're sweet. Thoughtful. Devious."

"You know me well." His grin might seem quick and relaxed, but she could see through it. He was nervous. "Does that mean you'll give me the answer I want?" he asked.

That mischievous and perverse streak in her tempted her to draw out this moment. To keep him on tenterhooks. But as she looked into his hopeful eyes, she simply couldn't do it to him. He'd been waiting patiently for her answer for six months, just as she'd demanded.

"Yes."

His arm tightened around her. "Which question are you answering? The one from just now, or the one from a six months ago?"

"Both."

He suddenly stopped their twirling movement across the dance floor, letting the other couples swirl past him. Then he picked her up and swung her around in his arms before pulling her close and kissing her soundly.

The other people on the dance floor seemed startled. Various expressions crossed the faces around them: surprise, shock, displeasure, even satisfaction.

Before Josephine could react, Frederick took her hand and hurried her off the dance floor and toward a side door.

"Where are you taking me?" she asked as he continued to pull her down the hallway. He glanced from side to side, as though he was searching for something.

They turned a corner and Frederick stopped in front of a pair of arched wooden doors. "Here," he said.

Before she could react, he pulled both doors wide and stepped into the small room.

He held one hand out to her, inviting her to join him, and the other hand gestured in a broad sweep across the room. "Your wedding, Lady Harrington."

Her hand flew to cover her mouth. She let out a gasp of surprise even as she reached out to clutch at Frederick's outstretched hand. Her mind swirled. She gripped his fingers tightly, holding on to that single piece of firm, solid reality in this swirling world.

She stood at the entrance of a small chapel. The soft glow of flickering candles illuminated the aisle and the man standing at the altar. The pastor.

She turned her gaze on Frederick. "You arranged all this? For me?"

"For us. I don't want to wait even one minute longer to marry you."

She took one step closer to him, then another. Then, they were standing shoulder to shoulder. She stood there for a moment, not moving. She absorbed the perfection of the moment, overwhelmed by it all.

Frederick tilted his head close to hers and murmured in her ear. "Is this what you want?"

Her breath hitched in her throat. She couldn't speak, so instead she gave a sharp, definitive nod.

He moved even closer, his voice even softer. "Then we should begin if we're still going to keep to our schedule for tonight."

She gave a soft gasp. "Our sch—"

She grabbed his hand, turned, and pulled him out the door and into the hallway. "Are you telling me we're still doing a mission? All of this wasn't a ruse simply to bring me here?"

A smile tugged at his mouth. "Truth has its price. I did promise not to lie to you."

She shook her head in bemusement. "Well, if this isn't proof of your commitment to honesty, I don't know what is." She looped her arm through his as she turned to face the chapel's entrance. "Let's get this over with. I'd hate to disrupt your plans."

He pulled her to a stop before she could rush them down the aisle. "No hurry. We're right on schedule."

She cocked an eyebrow at him. "By my calculations, we only have about ten minutes to complete this wedding."

He let out a sigh. "You never were good at studying my alternate plans."

She frowned at him. "The ones we're supposed to follow when things go wrong? You prepare so many of them, but we hardly ever use them."

He grinned. "This time, everything went right. Even so, we're using our alternative timetable tonight. That gives us a little over an hour before we need to slip away. Plenty of time to complete the ceremony and announce our marriage to everyone here at the embassy."

She narrowed her eyes. "Is that why you had three alternative plans for this mission?"

He glanced down at the floor. "I also thought having so many alternates would dissuade you from wanting to study them. I must admit, though, I had to have a plan in place in case you decided not to marry me."

She paused. "Four plans total?" She narrowed her eyes. "The one I already know about, right? A sort of a dummy plan that didn't include anything personal. That means there must have been a second one where my answer on the dance floor was yes, and a third one where I said no, right?"

A voice emerged from within the chapel. "Mr. Woolsy? Are you still in need of my services?"

Josephine glanced at the pastor and then back at Frederick.

"You mentioned you made three alternates to your original plan. Four in total. So what contingency did the forth one address?"

He swallowed. "This moment. It's the one I'll employ if my presumptuousness makes you change your answer. It's a rehashing of the plan where you rejected me on the ballroom floor. Neither one was pleasant to contemplate. They both include drunkenness, a tavern brawl, and the possibility of spending some time in a jail cell."

Behind his dry humor, she could see his love for her. It was right there in his eyes. Love, along with a bit of anxiety, as he waited for her decision.

Her heart swelled. She took a step forward, pulling him along with her. "Public drunkenness? You? Heaven forbid." She began walking down the aisle.

He fell in step beside her, his hand tightening around hers. "My future is in your hands. Do you know the power you hold over me?"

"The same power you hold over me."

And they walked into their future, together.

* * *

Want more romance, intrigue, and unforgettable characters?

Try GAMBLING ON A SCOUNDREL—a standalone historical romance from Sheridan Jeane.

Read GAMBLING ON A SCOUNDREL

* * *

The Secrets and Seduction series will continue with Along Came a Spy.

Join my VIP Club to be the first to hear when it releases.

* * *

My *Shadow of the Black Rose* trilogy, featuring Sir Frederick and Lady Josephine, is available from Dragonblade Publishing.

Read Book 1: WHISPERS AND SPIES

ALSO BY

Historical romances
By Sheridan Jeane
Gambling On a Scoundrel

Secrets and Seduction series:

It Takes a Spy...
Lady Catherine's Secret
Once Upon a Spy
My Lady, My Spy
Along Came a Spy

Also available:
Lady Cecilia Is Cordially Disinvited for Christmas
(only available via Sheridan's VIP club)

View the full Secrets and Seduction series and leave a review

Duke By Dawn (Novella, part of the anthology *Dukes All Night Long*)

The Shadow of the Black Rose - a Victorian-era Romantic Suspense trilogy
Whispers and Spies
The Spy In Disguise
Protect the Prince

Contemporary Romances
By Sheri Tyler
The Way to a Woman's Heart series - the **Coming Home** trilogy
Slow Simmer
Here's the Scoop
From Bitter to Sweet

The Way to a Woman's Heart series - the **Destination Wedding** trilogy
One Cup of Chemistry

ALSO BY

Say Cheese!
Kebabs and Kisses

ACKNOWLEDGMENTS

Thank you to Wendie Dikec for her fact checking assistance regarding Turkey in the 1850s.

Thank you to Caroline Norrington for her fabulous Scrivener template (affectionately referred to as "Caro's Template" in the Scrivener community).

Thank you as well to my beta readers, Pamela Jacques and Joe Ferguson.

ABOUT THE AUTHOR

Sheridan Jeane is an award-winning author of historical romantic suspense, weaving stories of intrigue, danger, and slow-burning romance. She also writes lighthearted contemporary romance under the name Sheri Tyler.

She grew up in Huber Heights, a suburb of Dayton, Ohio, and now lives just outside Pittsburgh. Sheridan holds a bachelor's degree in computer science with a minor in English. She co-founded Three Rivers Romance Writers, a former chapter of Romance Writers of America that supported a vibrant local community of romance writers.

When she's not reading or writing, she can be found learning to salsa dance, tumbling downhill on skis, or volunteering with the Child Health Association of Sewickley to support children in need in southwestern Pennsylvania.

www.SheridanJeane.com